LIVING LONG AGO

Felicity Brooks and Helen Edom

Edited by Cheryl Evans and Janet Cook

Designed by Mary Forster and Brian Robertson

Illustrated by Teri Gower, Guy Smith and Chris Lyon

Contents

Page 1   **Clothes and Fashion**

Page 25   **Homes and Houses**

Page 49   **Food and Eating**

Page 73   **Travel and Transport**

Page 97   **Index**

Series consultant: Dr Anne Millard
Language adviser: Betty Root M.B.E

CLOTHES AND FASHION

Consultant: Meg Douglas

Contents

2 The first clothes
4 Clothes in Ancient Egypt
6 Roman clothes
8 What the Vikings wore
10 Clothes in medieval times
12 European fashions
14 North American Indian clothes
16 French court fashions
18 Crinolines and corsets
20 Changing fashions
22 Clothes around the world
24 Clothes facts and dates

The first clothes

Clothes help to keep you warm and protect you from the sun and rain. They can also be nice to look at. Below you can find out about the first clothes people made.

The very first clothes were made from the skins of animals. People wrapped them around their bodies.

Mammoth

The skins came from animals such as mammoths, bison, deer and bears that people killed for food.

The skins helped people to keep warm but they were smelly, dirty and probably uncomfortable to wear.

Later people found out how to ▶ clean the skins. They stretched them out and scraped off the fat with stone scrapers.

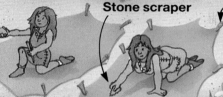

Stone scraper

Wooden pegs held the stretched skins in place on the ground.

Learning to sew

About 40,000 years ago people started to sew for the first time. ▶

A borer was also used to make holes in the skins. This made sewing easier. ▼

Thread was made from strips of animal gut or skin, ◀ or parts of plants.

The first needles were made out of ◀ thin pieces of bone or antler.

A tool called a borer was used to make holes in the needles.

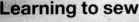

Borer

People could now sew skins together to make complicated clothes such as trousers and jackets.

2

Jewelry and decoration

The first jewelry was made from shells, small stones and animal teeth, bones and tusks.

Necklace made from carved mammoth tusk →

Shell necklace

Bear tooth necklace

▲ People also sewed shells and beads on their clothes. They probably made patterns on their bodies with a kind of red clay.

Make a 'mammoth tusk' necklace

You will need: eight corks, large needle, a skewer, 32 in piece of string.

Make a hole through each cork ▶ with the skewer.*

Thread the ◀ string through the needle.

Push the needle through the holes ▶ to thread the corks

Tie the ends of the string together.

Making skins soft

Skins had to be made soft before they could be cut. These are some of the ways this could be done.

◀ The skins were probably chewed.

They were ▶ soaked and beaten.

◀ They were rubbed with oil or fat.

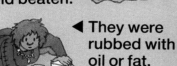

Later, skins were made into leather by soaking them in a liquid made from the bark of trees.

Weaving clothes

People first kept sheep about 10,000 years ago. They found out how to weave wool into cloth. They could also make linen from a plant called flax.

Loom

Weaver

Spindle

Looms were first used about 9000 years ago.

Weights

◀ First they made the wool or flax into thread. This is called spinning.

They wove thread into cloth on a wooden frame called a loom. The loom held one set of threads in place. The weaver passed another thread in and out between them to make cloth.

Dyes

Dyes made from things like leaves, berries and ground up rocks were used to change the color of the cloth.

Clothes in Ancient Egypt

The Egyptians cared a lot about the way they looked. Rich people had beautiful clothes, jewelry, wigs, perfume and make-up. Egypt is a hot country so people wore light, comfortable clothes or nothing at all.

We know what the Egyptians wore from writing, wall paintings and clothes found in ancient tombs.

Loom

Most clothes were made of linen. This was made from flax plants. The cloth was woven on large looms.

Perfume

Egyptians wore a lot of perfume made from flowers or scented wood. They kept it in small jars.

For parties, they often wore cones made of perfumed grease on their heads. The cones melted slowly and smelt nice.

In a rich man's garden

Here are some Egyptians in a rich man's garden. You can see some of the clothes different people wore.

Most clothes were white, but pieces of cloth found in tombs show that Egyptians also wore colorful clothes. ▶

Cone of perfumed grease

◀ Dancing girls wore just a belt of beads.

In the summer, ◀ children often wore nothing. Many had shaved heads with just a single piece of long hair.

Men wore a pleated linen robe over a short skirt. They also wore jewelry.

Arm-band

Egyptian make-up

Men and women wore make-up. They put red on their lips and cheeks and grey, green, or black make-up called kohl around their eyes. They also wore eye-shadow.

Jewelry

Ancient Egyptian jewelry was made from things such as silver, gold, copper, glass jewels, shells and pretty stones from the desert.

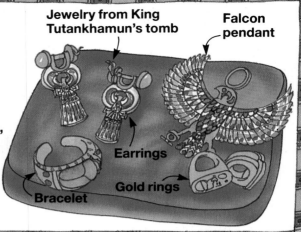

Jewelry from King Tutankhamun's tomb

Falcon pendant

Earrings

Gold rings

Bracelet

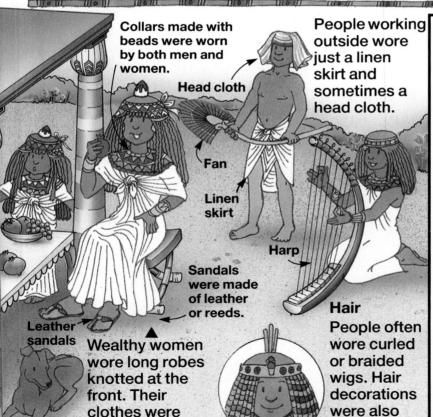

Collars made with beads were worn by both men and women.

Head cloth

Fan

Linen skirt

Harp

People working outside wore just a linen skirt and sometimes a head cloth.

Leather sandals

Sandals were made of leather or reeds.

Wealthy women wore long robes knotted at the front. Their clothes were finely pleated.

Hair

People often wore curled or braided wigs. Hair decorations were also popular.

Make an Egyptian collar

You will need:
Large piece of cardboard glue, gold or yellow paint pieces of colored foil, a skewer, string.

Cut out a half circle ▶ of cardboard.

← 11 in →

Cut it to this fan shape. Paint one side. ▶

Fan shape

3 in

When it is dry, ▶ stick on pieces of foil in rows.

Make two holes in ▶ the cardboard with the skewer.

Make ties with the ▶ string. Tie the collar around your neck.

5

Roman clothes

The Romans came from Italy and conquered many other countries. We know about what they wore from their statues, pictures and writing. Most clothes were made of wool or linen. Very rich people also had clothes of silk and cotton.

Getting dressed

Romans slept in their underwear or in their tunics when it was cold. Rich people had slaves to help them dress.

Women wore ▶ two pieces of underwear with a tunic on top.

Tunic

◀ Over this they wore a long dress called a stola and often a shawl called a palla.

Stola

Palla

Men wore a ▶ loincloth with a short tunic on top.

Tunic

Loincloth

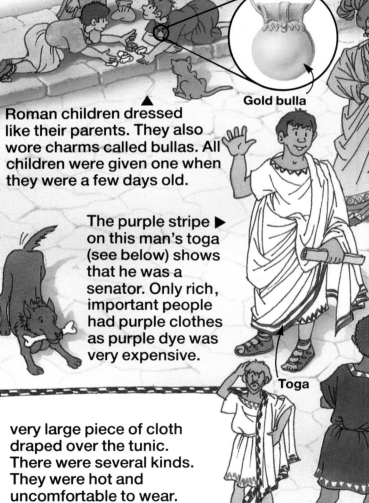

Roman children dressed like their parents. They also wore charms called bullas. All children were given one when they were a few days old.

Gold bulla

The purple stripe ▶ on this man's toga (see below) shows that he was a senator. Only rich, important people had purple clothes as purple dye was very expensive.

Toga

Togas

The people of Rome were divided into citizens and non-citizens. Only male citizens were allowed to wear togas. A toga was a very large piece of cloth draped over the tunic. There were several kinds. They were hot and uncomfortable to wear.

Fibula

People wore cloaks for travelling and when it was cold. Cloaks were fastened by a pin called a fibula.

The favorite colors for women's clothes were yellow, blue and red. Men often wore white. They had brightly colored clothes for parties.

This woman is on her way to the public baths. Her slave is carrying her make-up and perfume in a case.

Men wore ▶ dark-colored clothes when someone had died.

Soldiers' clothes

This is what a Roman soldier wore 1,900 years ago.

Metal helmet with pieces to protect the cheeks and neck

Woolen tunic with long sleeves

This scarf stopped the armor rubbing his neck.

Metal armor tied at the front

Shield made of wood, leather and iron

Spear

Leather sandals

Cleaning togas

Romans did not wash their togas, they sent them to a cleaner who was called a fuller.

He trod on them in water mixed with clay called fuller's earth. This cleaned them.

Wooden box

They were rinsed and then whitened over a fire burning sulphur, a chemical. They were brushed with hedgehog skins and pressed.

Shoes

Most shoes and boots were made of leather. You can see some below. Different shoes were worn indoors and outside. Romans going to a party took their indoor shoes with them.

What the Vikings wore

The Vikings came from Norway, Denmark and Sweden. In the winter it was very cold there, so everybody had warm clothes.

The men were fierce fighters so they also needed good weapons and clothes to protect them when they were fighting.

Women's clothes

Women spent a lot of time spinning and weaving inside their homes.

They wore a linen or wool dress with a tunic on top. The tunic was two pieces of cloth fastened with two oval brooches. ▶

Loom

They fixed chains to one of the brooches. They kept useful things such as knives, combs, purses and sewing and weaving tools on these chains.

They often wore a shawl or cloak made of wool or fur. ▼

Oval brooch

Silver chain

Woolen shawl

Woolen tunic

Soft sealskin shoes

Pleated linen dress

Woven pattern

Under their dresses they wore knee-length leggings and thick woolen socks when it was cold.

Viking combs

The Vikings made combs from deer antlers or bone. They used them often to comb their long hair. Combs were kept in bone comb cases.

Comb case **Antler comb**

Making cloth

Clothes were made from leather, fur, sheepskin, linen or wool. This is how woolen cloth was made.

▲ 1. The men cut the wool off the sheep with metal shears.

▲ 2. The women washed the wool in a stream to clean it.

8

▲ 3. They used iron combs to get rid of tangles in the wool.

▲ 4. They spun the wool into thread. Often they dyed it.

5. Thread was woven into cloth on a loom (see opposite page). Cloth was used for blankets, wall-hangings and clothes.

Men's clothes

Viking men wore tunics and various types of trousers. They also wore jewelry.

Cloak pin

Cap

Knife

Brooch

Cloth bands wrapped around legs

Most men wore their hair quite long. Small caps were popular. Fur hats were often worn in the winter. ▶

Belt with buckle

They had under-wear made of thin linen or wool.

Leather boots

Clothes for fighting

Viking men were very proud of being good fighters. They practiced often, starting when they were young boys.

Helmets often had metal pieces on the front to guard the face and make the fighter look more frightening.

Most men wore ▶ padded leather jackets. They sometimes had flat bones sewn inside to help give protection in battle.

Each man had a sword, a spear, an axe and a shield. Many of these weapons were decorated with silver and gold.

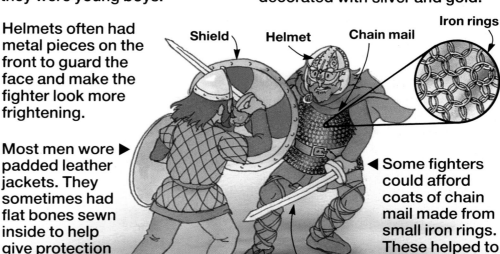

Shield

Helmet

Chain mail

Iron rings

Sword

◀ Some fighters could afford coats of chain mail made from small iron rings. These helped to protect them.

9

Clothes in medieval times

Fashions changed a lot during this time. Most people, however, could not afford new clothes, so their clothes stayed much the same. Only very wealthy people such as lords and ladies could afford to buy the latest fashions.

Putting on armor

A squire (a boy learning to be a knight) helped a knight to dress. Armor was expensive. Many squires couldn't afford it so they didn't become knights.

The knight put on a padded tunic and cap over his shirt.

He put on a chain mail shirt and hood (see page 9).

The squire strapped on a metal chest guard.

Next he strapped on leg, arm and shoulder guards.

Lastly he put on a metal helmet, spurs and a tunic with the knight's badge on it.

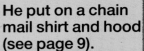

Later armor was so heavy, knights had to be pulled up on to horses with ropes.

In a rose garden

Rich people spent a lot of time in their gardens. Here you can see the way they dressed 570 years ago. Their clothes were made from expensive, embroidered cloth decorated with jewels and pearls.

Dagges

Dagges were a kind of medieval decoration. They were shapes cut into the edges of clothes. There were various kinds.

Horned head-dress

Wide sleeves with buttoned cuffs

Pouch

Knife

Hose

Men's leg ► coverings were called hose. They were like tights made of cloth. Sometimes each leg was a different color.

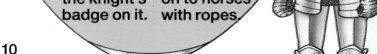

Wrapping babies

Babies were wrapped in bands of cloth. People believed this made their limbs grow straight. It was called swaddling.

Nearly everyone wore a hat. This kind was called a chaperon. ▼

Chaperon hat

Make a medieval pouch

Clothes did not have pockets so people kept things in pouches (little bags) tied around their waists.

To make a pouch you need: a circle of strong cloth (such as felt) 8 in across, scissors, a long piece of string.

Cut slits 1in apart near the edge of the circle. Do not cut through the edge. ▶

◀ Weave the string in and out through the slits.

Houppelande gown

This sort of gown was called a houppelande. This one has dagges ▶ on the sleeves.

Heart-shaped head-dress

Pull the ends of the ▶ string to gather the cloth into a pouch.

◀Women wore big head-dresses and robes with long sleeves. They wore their belts high up above their waists.

◀ You can now put things in the pouch and tie it around your waist.

Houses and castles were cold and drafty, so clothes were often lined with fur. This helped people to keep warm.

Fur lining

Shoe rules

Shoes with long toes were fashionable for many years. A law made in 1420 said that poor men were not allowed to wear them. A prince could wear shoes 24in long if he wanted.

Baggy tunic

Peasants' clothes

Peasants' clothes were made of ▶ rough linen or wool. They were looser than the rich people's clothes and better for working in.

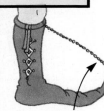

Some toes were tied to the legs so people didn't trip over.

European fashions

Fashions continued to change quickly during this time. The clothes people wore showed how rich and important they were.

Wealthy people took a lot of notice of what kings and queens wore at the court and often tried to copy them.

Even shoes had square toes.

Starting about 460 years ago, many men wore padded clothes which gave them a square shape.

Points

The different parts of a man's outfit were joined together with laces called points.

Women wore dresses with square-shaped necks. Head-dresses were built up around wire frames.

Corsets

Women started wearing corsets to make their waists look slim. Corsets were made from wood, whalebone, iron or steel. They were very tight and uncomfortable to wear. Children often wore them too.

Corset made of iron

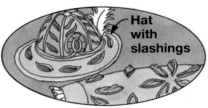

Older men, church men and university teachers wore long gowns. These were often lined with fur.

Hat with slashings

Slits, called slashings, were often cut in clothes to let the colorful lining show through.

A royal dance

These are the kind of clothes people wore for a court dance about 400 years ago.

Fashionable moustache and small pointed beard

Men carried a sword or dagger.

Men and women wore earrings.

Musician

Ruff

◀ Separate collars made from folded linen were called ruffs.

Farthingales

Skirts were held out by frames called farthingales. The frames were made of whalebone, wood, wire or padding covered in linen. There were three main types:

The Spanish farthingale was shaped like a cone.

The wheel farthingale was round.

The roll farthingale was worn around the hips. It was tied at the front.

How to make a ruff

Ruffs were very popular. Some were so large that people needed spoons with very long handles to reach their mouths to eat.

To make a ruff you need: two large pieces of paper, cellophane tape, scissors, two paper clips.

◀ Cut out two large circles of paper.

12 in

Mark a small ▶ circle in the center of each.

◀3 in▶

◀ Cut into the big circles and cut out the small circles.

Fold each big ▶ circle like a fan as shown here.

Tape

◀ Tape the two parts of the ruff together.

Put the ruff on. ▶ Ask a friend to join the ends with paperclips.

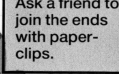

Hats were worn indoors and outside. Flat hats decorated with feathers were popular. ▼

Stiff top called a bodice

Padded sleeves

Round-toed shoes with flat heels

Full patterned skirt over a farthingale

Men wore cloaks of velvet, leather and other materials. Some men ◀ had three, for the morning, afternoon and evening.

Padded breeches, called trunk hose

◀ Men's leg coverings, or hose, were now knitted from wool or silk.

Padded velvet top called a doublet

North American Indian clothes

Many Indian tribes lived in North America. Each tribe had its own style of clothes and jewelry. These are the clothes worn by the North-east Woodlands tribes.

This is where the North-east Woodlands tribes lived.

Moccasins

Indians wore leather shoes called moccasins. Each tribe made and decorated them in a different way. Some were made from only one piece of soft leather.

These flaps protected the ankles from snake and insect bites.

Hair in braids

Baby wrapped in skins and fur

Leather top decorated with beads and laces

Bracelets

Decorated leather skirt

Moccasins

Deerskin leggings tied below the knees protected the legs from bites.

Beads

Indians made beads from shells, bones, claws and stones. Later they also used glass beads brought by Europeans.

Necklace made from shells

Colorful clothes

About 350 years ago, many rich Europeans wore colorful, expensive clothes. These were made of cloth such as satin and silk. Lace, ribbons and feathers were popular.

Pearl necklaces

Big lacy collar

Wide sleeves with lace cuffs

Long velvet gown decorated with gold thread

Satin dress

Skirt held out by layers of petticoats

Large hat with feathers

Long curled hair

Lace-edged collar called a falling band

Cloak

Long doublet

Sword

Knee-length breeches

High leather boots with wide tops

Spurs

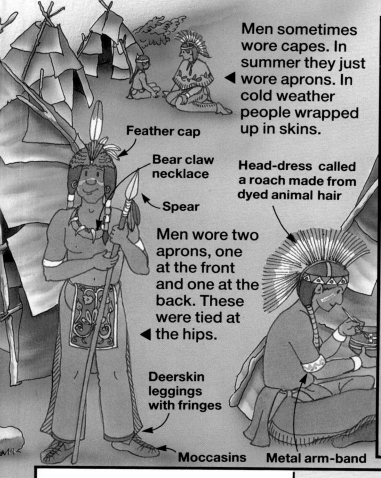

Men sometimes wore capes. In summer they just wore aprons. In cold weather people wrapped up in skins.

Feather cap

Bear claw necklace

Spear

Head-dress called a roach made from dyed animal hair

Men wore two aprons, one at the front and one at the back. These were tied at the hips.

Deerskin leggings with fringes

Moccasins   **Metal arm-band**

Puritan clothes

Some people in Europe believed it was wicked to wear brightly colored and decorated clothes. Those living in England were called Puritans. Some of them went to live in America in 1620. These are the kind of plain clothes they wore.

Small linen cap

Starched white collar

Long skirt worn over another skirt and layers of petticoats

Apron

Children were dressed like their parents.

Tall 'sugar loaf' hat

Puritan men were not allowed to have long hair.

Breeches

Stockings

Low-heeled shoes

Patches and masks

Some people in Europe wore patches on their faces. These were made of velvet or silk. People started to do this to hide scars and pimples. Then it became fashionable.

Some women wore masks. These were to keep out the sun or as a disguise.

Horse and carriage

How to make a beauty patch

You will need:
black paper,
scissors,
white crayon,
half a tea-
spoon of flour,
few drops
of water.

1. Draw a heart, star or other shape on the paper. ▶

2. Cut the shape out with ▶ the scissors.

3. Mix the flour and water ▶ to make a sticky paste.

4. Stick the patch on your ▶ face with the paste.

French court fashions

The French court was the center of European fashion at this time. Rich people's clothes were mostly made of silk and were very expensive. They were often decorated with beautiful embroidery, jewels, lace and ribbons.

At home

At home, men took off their wigs and jackets and relaxed in a dressing gown and cap. Their own hair was shaved or very short. Women wore a loose gown and no corset.

Wig on wig stand

Spraying powder on a wig

Dressing took a long time.

Dirtiness

Most people did not wash very often. King Louis XIV took a bath only once a year. People just wiped their faces and hands on a cloth and used a lot of perfume.

▶ Some women had young African boys as servants. They wore the same clothes as French men but with a turban.

Turban

Stomacher decorated with bows

Painted fan from China

Tight breeches

Silk stockings

Skirts were held out at the sides by frames called paniers. Some were so wide, women had to turn ▶ sideways to get through doorways.

◀ Under their dresses women wore corsets to make them look slim. Dresses had a stiff panel called a stomacher at the front.

Pockets

Pockets were little flat bags tied around the waist. They were not sewn into dresses. Women reached them through slits in their skirts.

Pockets

Make-up

People wore a lot of thick make-up. They used white to cover scars and make them look pale. They put red on their cheeks.

Men's wigs

Men wore wigs made of human, goat or horse hair. Human hair was the most expensive. Wigs were often covered in powder. There were many kinds.

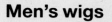

Tie wig of 1740 →

Most people didn't ▶ clean their teeth so many had bad teeth. False ones were made of ivory, bone, china or even wood.

Silk shirt with frilly cuffs

Long coat with wide bottom

Hat with three corners called a tricorne hat

Leather shoes with silver buckles

Enormous hair-styles

In the 1770s and 80s women had big hair-styles. Their own hair and false hair were combed over pads or wire frames and held in place with hairpins and grease.

Some styles were three feet high.

Women used ivory sticks to scratch their itchy heads.

Decorations such as feathers, flowers and even model ships were put on top.

The hair was covered in scented powder.

It took hours to do these styles. The hair was then not touched for weeks. It often became the home of lice and fleas.

Waistcoats

Waistcoat fronts were made of silk covered in embroidery. The backs were made of cheaper material. Waistcoats were fastened by gold or jeweled buttons.

The French Revolution

In 1789, the poorer people of France rebelled and seized power from the rich people. This was called the French Revolution. These are the kind of simple clothes the rebels wore. After the Revolution everyone wore much simpler styles.

The colors of the new French flag were red, white and blue. These colors were also used for clothes.

Hat called a Phrygian cap

Red, white and blue rosette

The rebels wore trousers instead of breeches.

Long pike

Red sash

Wooden shoes

Crinolines and corsets

At the beginning of the nineteenth century, womens's clothes were quite simple. Over the next hundred years, styles changed many times. Men's clothes changed less but various materials and colors were used.

Top hat

In 1800, women's dresses had a high waist. They were made of thin, light material. Men wore coats, waistcoats and trousers instead of breeches.

1800

Bonnet

1835

1855

1865

1875

1885

1895

Amelia Bloomer

Amelia Bloomer was an American. In the 1850s she tried to persuade women to wear loose, comfortable clothes.

Bloomers

People thought her baggy trousers, or bloomers, were shocking. Forty years later, women began to wear them for cycling.

Skirts got wider and wider until 1865. At first they were held out by petticoats. Later they used frames called crinolines. After 1865, skirts were full at the back and straight at the front.

Crinoline dangers

There were many dangers and problems in wearing crinolines. Here are some of them.

◀ It was easy to knock things off shelves and tables as you walked past.

◀ Strong winds could blow you off your feet.

It was hard to lie down and difficult to get up if you fell over.

Skirts caught fire easily if you ◀ stood too close to an open fire.

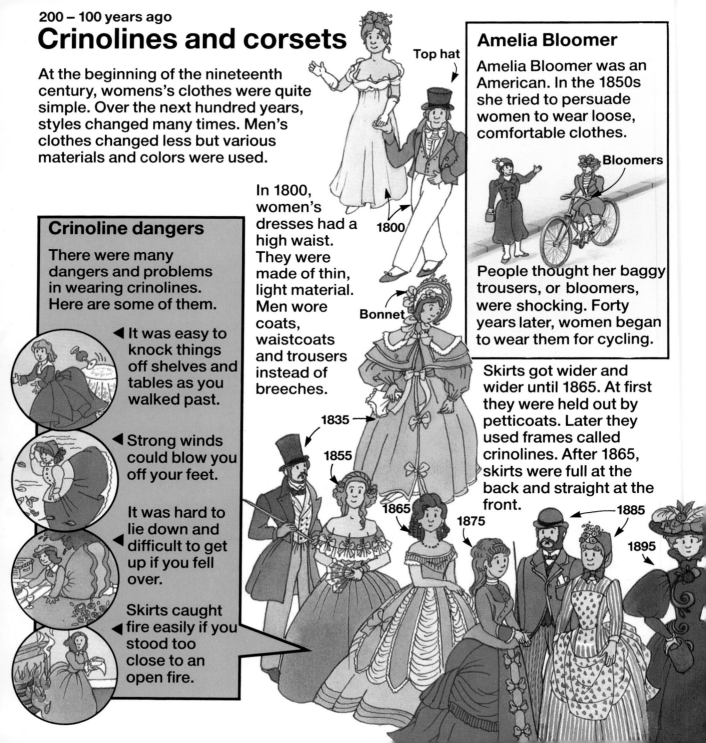

Fashion in photographs

In 1851 a camera was invented that could take cheap, good quality photographs. All sorts of people could now afford to have their picture taken at a studio.

Collections of these pictures still survive. From them we know a lot about what people wore. ▶

People had to keep very still to have their ▶ picture taken, so they often look rather stiff.

Milk woman in 1872

Camera

Fashion extras

Here are some of the extra things that women wore or needed to help them look after their clothes.

Soft leather gloves

Glove stretchers for pulling fingers of gloves into shape

Buttonhook for doing up buttons

Hat-pin for keeping hats on

Fan

Type of glasses called lorgnettes

Purse (handbags weren't used until about 1880).

Corsets

Women's corsets were laced up very tightly indeed. The ideal waist measurement was thought to be 18in or less. Girls wore corsets from about the age of eleven.

Tying a corset

Crinoline

Corset dangers

Doctors warned that it was dangerous to squash the body in corsets. Women took little notice and often fainted because they found it hard to breathe.

Children's clothes

Until they were about ▶ five, boys wore dresses. When they were older they wore suits with breeches or trousers, and hats.

Boys' clothes

Under their skirts, girls often wore pantalettes. These were tubes of white linen edged with lace. They were tied on to a waistband.

Pantalettes

Changing fashions

Clothes can change a lot during a century. Here you can see some of the many different styles that have been popular since 1900.

1900

Big hat with feathers

Soft leather gloves

Parasol

Men always wore hats out of doors. Top hats, straw hats, and caps were popular.

Young girls wore their long hair loose.

Buttoned boots

Women wore a new kind of corset which gave them an 'S' shaped figure. Their long skirts flared out at the bottom.

Car clothes

Early cars did not have a roof. People wore gloves, 'dust coats' or rain coats, hats with veils, or caps and goggles. These helped to protect them from rain, cold, dirt and dust.

1910

Women began wearing skirts that were so narrow at the bottom that they could only take tiny steps. These were called 'hobble skirts'.

Very large hat

Long gloves

Hobble skirt

Clothes were often decorated with buttons.

Parasol

1914–1918 Uniforms

At the start of World War One, many men wanted to become soldiers. People liked their smart uniforms. As the war went on, many men were killed or injured. Uniforms were no longer so much admired.

American soldier 1918

1920s

Women's clothes changed completely in the 1920s. The new short skirts and hairstyles were thought to be very daring.

Straight dress with a very low waist

Hat called a cloche

1930s

Going to the movies was popular. Some people tried to copy the styles film stars wore. Most people could not afford these styles.

Trilby hat

Striped suit

Black and white shoes

Beach clothes

In the 1930s, sunbathing first became fashionable. Before that time beach clothes had covered up a lot of the body.

1905   1931   1954   1970

Jeans

The first jeans were made in America in 1874. They were strong trousers for working men. American students first wore them in the 1940s.

Jeans are still very popular.

1939 – 1945 War clothes

War-time suit 1942

Soldier's uniform

Working clothes

In Europe during World War Two, material was hard to buy. Clothes were made which did not use much material. In America, it was easier to buy the latest fashions and nylon stockings (a new invention).

1950s

In the 1950s, women enjoyed wearing full skirts again. These were held out by petticoats. They used a lot of material.

Dress with a tight top and narrow waist

Full skirt held out by petticoats

Teenage clothes

Before the 1950s, teenagers wore similar clothes to adults. In the 1950s, they began to dress in their own way. They copied some styles from rock 'n' roll singers.

1960s

In the 1960s, new materials such as plastic, metal and even paper were used for clothes.

Mini skirts were first worn in 1965.

Women first wore tights in the 1960s.

More changes

There have been many more styles since the 1960s. These are two of them.

Many styles such as punk have come from pop music. Punk started in 1976.

1960s and 70s hippy clothes

Clothes around the world

All over the world, people wear different styles of clothes. The way people dress depends on what materials they have and what the weather is like where they live. The clothes you can see below have changed little over many years.

Silk secret

Silk is a beautiful, soft material. The Chinese discovered how to make it thousands of years ago. They kept their discovery secret for centuries. Anybody who told the secret to a foreigner was executed.

Silk is made from threads that silkworms spin around their bodies to make → a cocoon.

Dragon robes

Important people in China used to wear long silk robes. Many had dragons embroidered on them in silver, gold and colored thread.

Dragon robe from 200 years ago

Japanese kimonos

In Japan, people have ▶ been wearing gowns called kimonos for over a thousand years. With the kimono they wear a wide sash called an obi around their waists. It is tied at the back in a special way.

Obi

Kimono

Sari

Choli

The hands of a Hindu bride are decorated with henna (a dye). →

Nigerian clothes

Some women in ▶ Nigeria now wear Western clothes but many keep their traditional clothes. These are patterned cotton dresses and head-dresses.

Indian saris

◀ A modern sari is a piece of material three feet wide and 18 feet long. Saris have been worn in India, Pakistan and Bangladesh for hundreds of years.

There are several ways of wrapping a sari around your body. A small top called a choli is worn underneath.

Clothes in Lapland

People who live in Lapland ▶ are called Sámis. Because it is very cold, they wear warm clothes made from wool and reindeer skins. These styles have hardly changed for many years.

Clothes in Peru

◀ Indians in Peru in South America weave their clothes from sheep and llama wool. In winter women wear several skirts to keep warm.

American cowboys

Modern cowboys' clothes are very similar to those worn a hundred years ago.

Hat called a stetson →

Neckerchief protects against dust

Waistcoat

Cotton shirt

Jeans

Leather leggings called chaps

Lasso

Leather boots with heels

Clothes from plants

Here are some of the ways people use plants to make clothes.

Many tribes weave leaves to make into loincloths and aprons.

In Fiji a cloth called masi is made from bark.

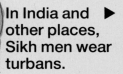

In Mexico, a material called ixtle is made from a tough cactus.

Hats and head-dresses

Here are some of the hats and head-dresses people in different countries wear.

These grass ▶ hats are worn in Lesotho, Southern Africa. They are called mokorotlo.

Arabic ▶ kaffiyehs are made of linen, cotton, wool or silk. They are held in place by a band called an egal.

Kaffiyeh

Egal

Embroidered ▶ hats are worn by boys in Afghanistan.

In India and ▶ other places, Sikh men wear turbans.

In the Far East people wear straw hats to protect them from the sun. ▶

Clothes facts and dates

Earliest armor

★The earliest known armor was made in Mesopotamia about 4000 years ago. It was made up of hundreds of small pieces of bronze.

First class mail

★A coat of chain mail (see pages 9 and 10) could be made of over 200,000 rings and weigh nearly 60 pounds (27 kilograms).

★Chain mail often became rusty in the rain. One way of getting rid of rust was to put the mail into a leather bag with sand and vinegar and throw it around like a ball.

Medieval clothes laws

★In medieval times, only nobles could wear fine furs. Poorer people were only allowed dog, cat, badger or fox fur.

★In Germany, only nobles were allowed to wear red clothes.

★In France, the church said people should not wear long pointed shoes since it stopped them from being able to kneel and pray.

★In England, a law of 1475 said that anybody except a lord, esquire or gentlemen, who wore a coat that didn't cover his bottom would have to pay a fine of 20 shillings.

Tall stories

★The very tall hair-styles worn by women in the 1770s and 80s (see page 17) gave them many problems. Here are some of them:

– The hair caught fire if women walked into chandeliers (see page 41).

–They had to sleep sitting up so that they didn't disturb their hair.

– Doors at the palace of Versailles (see page 48) had to be made taller so hair-styles would fit through.

Water worries

★A book on good behavior published in France in 1749 said that it was a bad idea to wash since this made you more likely to get colds in winter and sunburn in summer.

Wig tales

★These are some of the names of different kinds of wigs worn by men (see page 17) in the eighteenth century: Elephant, Buzz, Prudence puff, Rhinoceros, Fox ear, Rose bag, Scratch, She-dragon and Staircase.

Skirt crimes

★In the 1920s, people tried to pass laws to stop women wearing short skirts. In Utah, U.S.A, any woman wearing a skirt higher than three inches (seven and a half centimetres) above the ankle could be fined or put in prison.

HOMES AND HOUSES

Consultants: Simon and Julie Penn, Avoncroft Museum

Contents

26 Caves and shelters
28 An Ancient Egyptian villa
30 A Roman town house
32 A Viking long house
34 A castle
36 A town house in North Europe
38 Dutch merchants' houses
40 A French nobleman's home
42 Homes in the Wild West
44 Terraced houses
46 Other types of houses
48 Facts about homes

Caves and shelters

The first people did not live in one place all year. In summer they slept in shelters made from branches. In winter they stayed in caves. Once a family found a good, dry cave they returned to the same one every year when the weather grew cold.

A cave home in winter

Caves gave good shelter from winter storms. People burned fires inside for warmth and light. They also used lamps so they could see to make tools or mend clothes.

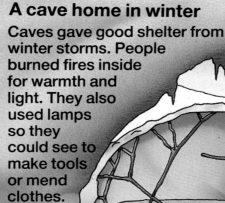

People killed wild animals for meat.

Trash pile

A woman sewing.

A skin wind-break helps keep out the wind.

This man carves a bone with a flint. He is making a harpoon or fish spear.

This man is feeding the fire with branches.

They lit fires by striking sparks from sharp stones called flints. Once a fire was lit it was kept burning day and night.

Summer homes

This man is smearing mud over the branches to keep out rain.

A reindeer skin covers the doorway.

In summer people moved around to follow the animals they hunted for meat. Each time, they built new shelters using branches found nearby.

Mammoth huts

On the Russian plains people made huts from the skins and bones of mammoths. These were animals like huge, hairy elephants that they hunted for food. There were no caves on the plains so people lived in mammoth huts all year.

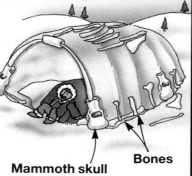

Mammoth skull

Bones

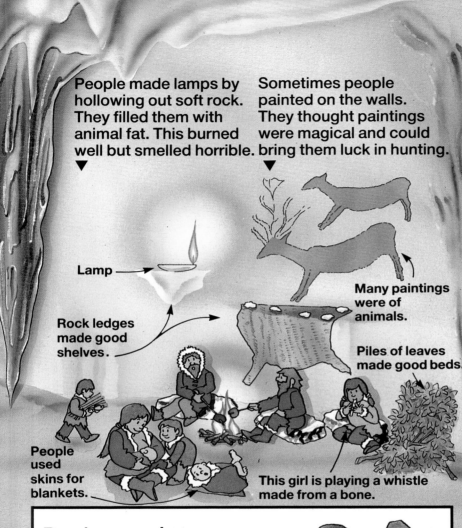

People made lamps by hollowing out soft rock. They filled them with animal fat. This burned well but smelled horrible. ▼

Sometimes people painted on the walls. They thought paintings were magical and could bring them luck in hunting. ▼

Lamp →

Rock ledges made good shelves.

Many paintings were of animals.

Piles of leaves made good beds.

People used skins for blankets.

This girl is playing a whistle made from a bone.

Cave paintings

Paints were mixed on a flat stone.

Reed

Feather

▲ Cave painters used twigs, reeds or feathers instead of brushes. They made paint by grinding up colored rocks and mixing them with fat.

▲ Some of them made pictures by placing their hands on the wall. They blew paint around them through a reed.

Try it yourself

Do this on a large piece of paper. Use powder paint mixed with water.

▲ Dip a straw in a jar of paint. Press your tongue over the hole in the straw. Lift the straw and blow the paint around your hand.

Burying people

When people died they were often buried in the earth floor of a cave home. The family put the dead person's belongings in the grave. They scattered flowers before covering the body with earth.

An Ancient Egyptian villa

The Egyptians lived by the River Nile. They dug mud from its banks and used it to make bricks to build houses. These mud houses stayed cool in Egypt's hot, dry weather.

This big house is called a villa. It was part of a large farm. Some farm buildings were inside its courtyard.

People often went out on to the roof as it was cool and breezy. There were leather shades to keep off the sun.

Shade made of pieces of leather stitched together.

Animal pen

Courtyard

This servant is fetching water from the well for the house.

These are called hieroglyphics. They spell the owner's name in Egyptian writing.

This step helped to stop snakes climbing inside.

Well

The gardener had to water the plants a lot to make them grow.

People were proud of their gardens. They rested and played games in them.

Garden pool

Board game

How do we know?

Over many years, old houses crumble away. They become buried in earth with other things people used.

Today, archaeologists dig for remains and piece them together. Things left in pyramids (see right) also give clues to the past.

Inside the house

Inside, the villa was colorful. There were painted walls and columns, and decorated furniture. Here are some things Egyptians had in their homes about 3,500 years ago.

This part of the column is carved to look like an Egyptian flower called a lotus.

Real lotus bud

These reed baskets were used instead of cupboards.

Pictures like this were painted on the walls.

This furniture is decorated with animal carvings.

Lion's claws

Duck heads

Fan made of feathers.

People took showers in wash-rooms by getting servants to pour water over them. ▶

Stones to stop mud walls getting wet.

Water runs away along here.

The toilet was a wooden seat fixed over a pot. The pot was full of sand. ▼

Pot

Hippopotamus toy

Reed window coverings kept out the sun.

Bins for storing grain.

Pyramids

Egyptians thought a dead person's spirit could visit its body so they preserved bodies with chemicals.

Mummy (preserved body)

Building a pyramid

Secret chamber

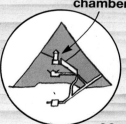

Around 4,500 years ago, Egyptian pharaohs (kings) built pyramids. Their bodies were buried in them when they died.

The pharaoh's body was laid in a secret chamber. Games, furniture and jewels were put with the body for its spirit to use.

Egyptian pets

Egyptians kept cats and dogs in their homes. They trained both to help them hunt birds and animals.

When a cat died, its owner shaved off half an eyebrow to show how upset she was.

A Roman town house

Roman houses were designed to stay cool in Italy's* hot sun. The rooms were grouped around an open courtyard called an atrium. This let in lots of light and air.

Heat and light

In cold weather, Romans burned a fire in a pit under the ground floor. The smoke and heat spread beneath the floor and warmed the rooms.

This kind of heating was called a hypocaust.

Wick

At night, they burned oil in lamps to light their rooms.

Oil went in here

Flushing toilets

The Romans were very clean. They took lots of baths and had flushing toilets.

A drain took waste out of the house (see right).

People tipped water into the toilet to flush it.

They used sponges, not paper.

Water jar

Hole

Stone seat

Houses were built of brick. The walls were covered with smooth plaster.

Roofs sloped so rain could run off them. They were covered in clay tiles.

Walls were painted pale colors to help keep the house cool.

Tiles

Pillars helped to hold up the roof.

Couch

Owner's bedroom

Jars of skin cream

People used the garden as an extra living room in hot weather.

Garden

clavdiv

People sometimes wrote things on house walls although it annoyed the owner.

Owner's study

Mosaic

Floors often had patterns called mosaics on them. They were made by sticking colored stones into plaster.

*The Romans came from Italy.

A rich family's house had many rooms for eating, sleeping and living, and separate rooms for slaves. It had a garden and even running water. Not everyone was so lucky. A poor family had to live in one room in a block with lots of other people.

A rich family's house

Atrium

Most windows and doors opened on to the atrium.

Shutters could be closed to keep out the sun.

Rich people often had shops at the front of their houses. They paid servants to run them. ▼

Slaves' bedroom

A slave called a porter and his dog guarded this entrance.

Wall painting

Chest for clothes

Mattress

Streets were paved with flat stones.

Lamp-stand

Rain water fell here.

Statue of god

Smoke from fire in kitchen

Porter's lodge

The Romans laid pipes and drains underground.

Pipe took fresh water to house.

▲
Romans had many gods. They thought some watched over homes. They kept statues of them inside.

Dirty water flowed away.

Drain

A Viking long house

The Vikings were people from Norway, Sweden and Denmark. They sailed to many countries; sometimes to raid them but often to trade, or swap goods, with the people there. Many Vikings settled in the foreign lands they visited.

Buried treasure

Chiefs often got rich by trading or raiding. They buried their treasure in secret places. Even now people sometimes find hidden Viking treasure.

Story-telling

Vikings told stories about giants and gods. They made them into poems so they were easier to remember. They paid poets to tell them at feasts.

People had to fetch all their water from this stream.

A chief's house was up to 100 feet long. That is longer than a tennis court.

Vikings were good carpenters. They built most houses out of wood.

Wooden beams were often decorated with carved patterns.

This house is in Norway which has cold, snowy winters.

Man carving walrus tusk.

This straw roof covering is called thatch.

A salt peddler is visiting the chief. His men guard his goods.

Slaves like this one were often captured in raids.

Logs for fire inside

A Viking chief's home was called a long house. All his family and slaves lived with him. He left them at home when he went with his men on expeditions.

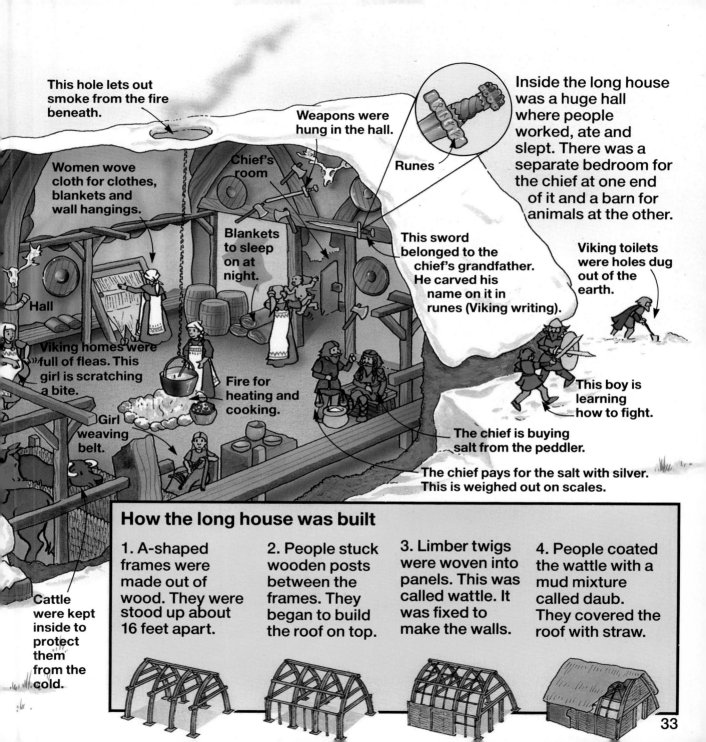

This hole lets out smoke from the fire beneath.

Women wove cloth for clothes, blankets and wall hangings.

Weapons were hung in the hall.

Chief's room

Runes

Inside the long house was a huge hall where people worked, ate and slept. There was a separate bedroom for the chief at one end of it and a barn for animals at the other.

Blankets to sleep on at night.

This sword belonged to the chief's grandfather. He carved his name on it in runes (Viking writing).

Hall

Viking toilets were holes dug out of the earth.

Viking homes were full of fleas. This girl is scratching a bite.

Fire for heating and cooking.

Girl weaving belt.

This boy is learning how to fight.

The chief is buying salt from the peddler.

The chief pays for the salt with silver. This is weighed out on scales.

Cattle were kept inside to protect them from the cold.

How the long house was built

1. A-shaped frames were made out of wood. They were stood up about 16 feet apart.

2. People stuck wooden posts between the frames. They began to build the roof on top.

3. Limber twigs were woven into panels. This was called wattle. It was fixed to make the walls.

4. People coated the wattle with a mud mixture called daub. They covered the roof with straw.

33

A castle

In Europe at this time, rich and powerful lords fought each other a great deal. They built strong castles to stop enemies stealing their property.

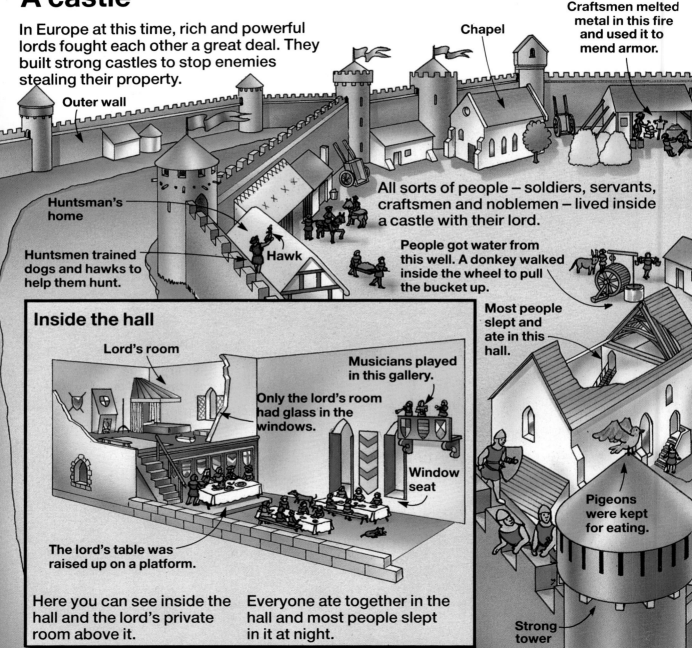

Chapel

Craftsmen melted metal in this fire and used it to mend armor.

Outer wall

Huntsman's home

Huntsmen trained dogs and hawks to help them hunt.

Hawk

All sorts of people – soldiers, servants, craftsmen and noblemen – lived inside a castle with their lord.

People got water from this well. A donkey walked inside the wheel to pull the bucket up.

Most people slept and ate in this hall.

Inside the hall

Lord's room

Musicians played in this gallery.

Only the lord's room had glass in the windows.

Window seat

Pigeons were kept for eating.

The lord's table was raised up on a platform.

Here you can see inside the hall and the lord's private room above it.

Everyone ate together in the hall and most people slept in it at night.

Strong tower

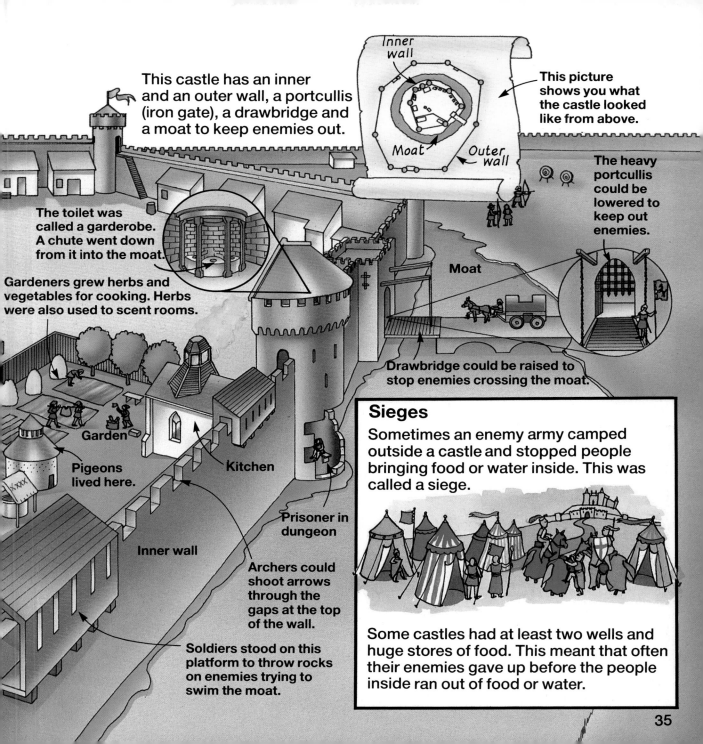

This castle has an inner and an outer wall, a portcullis (iron gate), a drawbridge and a moat to keep enemies out.

Inner wall

This picture shows you what the castle looked like from above.

Moat

Outer wall

The heavy portcullis could be lowered to keep out enemies.

The toilet was called a garderobe. A chute went down from it into the moat.

Gardeners grew herbs and vegetables for cooking. Herbs were also used to scent rooms.

Moat

Drawbridge could be raised to stop enemies crossing the moat.

Garden

Pigeons lived here.

Kitchen

Inner wall

Prisoner in dungeon

Archers could shoot arrows through the gaps at the top of the wall.

Soldiers stood on this platform to throw rocks on enemies trying to swim the moat.

Sieges

Sometimes an enemy army camped outside a castle and stopped people bringing food or water inside. This was called a siege.

Some castles had at least two wells and huge stores of food. This meant that often their enemies gave up before the people inside ran out of food or water.

35

A town house in North Europe

Towns were crowded, dirty places. People lived in small houses, built close together.

Many families worked in their homes as well as lived there. Below you can see a house where they made woollen cloth.

Smoke gets out through this covered hole.

Smoke from the fire goes up to the roof.

Windows

Glass windows were expensive. People mostly used other things to cover the holes, as you can see below.

Cloth dipped in clear oil let some light in and kept the wind out.

Criss-crossed wood let lots of light in and kept out most of the wind.

Bars kept some wind out. Shutters were closed over them in cold weather.

People prayed at home every day.

The house has a ▶ frame of wooden beams. The walls are fixed in between. They are made of wattle and daub (see page 33).

At night the rooms were lit with candles.

Kitchen

The mother is washing sheep's wool.

Streets had open drains. They were often blocked with smelly garbage.

The house had three rooms. The back one was a kitchen. Most of it was open to the roof.

The roof is covered in clay tiles.

This room was a bedroom and living room. Here the daughters combed and spun wool before it was woven into cloth. ▼

One girl is combing wool to untangle it.

This girl is spinning wool.

Everyone sleeps in this room. Smaller beds were kept under here.

Baby in cradle

Spare wool was kept in chests.

A customer looks at some cloth.

This was a workshop. Here the father wove wool into cloth on a loom. ▼

Loom

Boy winding thread.

Money bag

A boot-maker's sign

Most people fetched water from a pump.

Garbage was often thrown in the street.

Buying water

Pump water was often dirty. Water-sellers carried fresh water from springs for rich people to buy. Some tricked people by filling buckets with dirty water from town pumps.

Taking baths

Wooden tub

People only bathed about once a year as they thought it could make them ill. Some rested in bed after a bath to help them recover.

Dutch merchants' houses

At this time there were many merchants in Europe. They were people who bought and sold goods. Some sent ships to fetch things from places as far away as China. They sold these things for lots of money.

Holland had good ships so there were a lot of rich merchants there. Here you can see merchants' houses in Amsterdam, an important city in Holland.

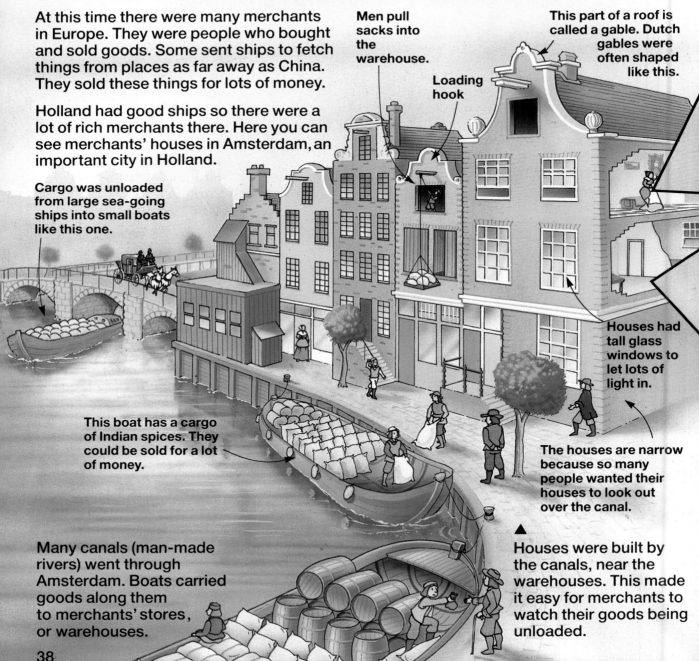

Men pull sacks into the warehouse.

Loading hook

This part of a roof is called a gable. Dutch gables were often shaped like this.

Cargo was unloaded from large sea-going ships into small boats like this one.

Houses had tall glass windows to let lots of light in.

This boat has a cargo of Indian spices. They could be sold for a lot of money.

The houses are narrow because so many people wanted their houses to look out over the canal.

▲ Houses were built by the canals, near the warehouses. This made it easy for merchants to watch their goods being unloaded.

Many canals (man-made rivers) went through Amsterdam. Boats carried goods along them to merchants' stores, or warehouses.

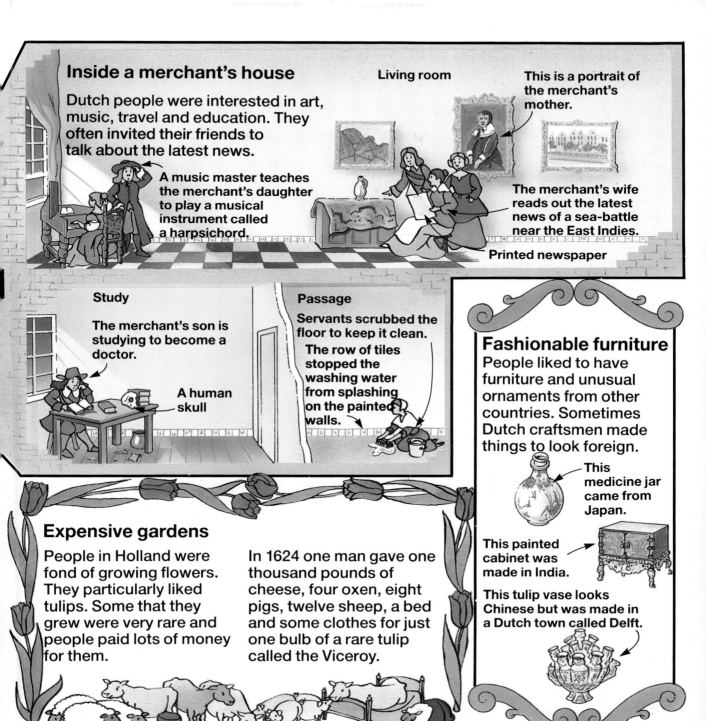

Inside a merchant's house

Dutch people were interested in art, music, travel and education. They often invited their friends to talk about the latest news.

A music master teaches the merchant's daughter to play a musical instrument called a harpsichord.

Living room

This is a portrait of the merchant's mother.

The merchant's wife reads out the latest news of a sea-battle near the East Indies.

Printed newspaper

Study

The merchant's son is studying to become a doctor.

A human skull

Passage

Servants scrubbed the floor to keep it clean.

The row of tiles stopped the washing water from splashing on the painted walls.

Fashionable furniture

People liked to have furniture and unusual ornaments from other countries. Sometimes Dutch craftsmen made things to look foreign.

This medicine jar came from Japan.

This painted cabinet was made in India.

This tulip vase looks Chinese but was made in a Dutch town called Delft.

Expensive gardens

People in Holland were fond of growing flowers. They particularly liked tulips. Some that they grew were very rare and people paid lots of money for them.

In 1624 one man gave one thousand pounds of cheese, four oxen, eight pigs, twelve sheep, a bed and some clothes for just one bulb of a rare tulip called the Viceroy.

A French nobleman's home

In France, two hundred and fifty years ago, most people had to work very hard to earn their living. But a few people were very rich and hardly worked at all. They lived in luxury in big houses and were looked after by lots of servants.

This house belongs to a rich nobleman.

French builders copied parts of Ancient Greek and Roman buildings to make houses look grand.

This part is built to look like a Greek temple.

Chimney sweeps

Chimneys often got blocked with soot. Young children were paid to climb up them to brush them out. This was dangerous. Many fell and were killed.

Gardens were planned to be beautiful and interesting to walk in.

The plants in these flower beds are meant to make them look like cards.

The French Revolution

In 1789 the poor in France rebelled against rich and powerful people. They turned nobles out of their homes and took away their property and power. This was called the French Revolution.

Rebels

Inside a lady's bedroom

A rich lady often had visitors while she finished dressing in her bedroom.

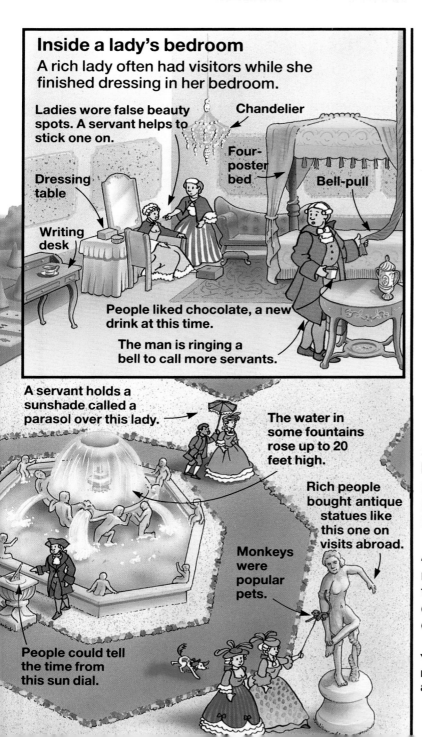

Ladies wore false beauty spots. A servant helps to stick one on.

Chandelier

Four-poster bed

Bell-pull

Dressing table

Writing desk

People liked chocolate, a new drink at this time.

The man is ringing a bell to call more servants.

A servant holds a sunshade called a parasol over this lady.

The water in some fountains rose up to 20 feet high.

Rich people bought antique statues like this one on visits abroad.

Monkeys were popular pets.

People could tell the time from this sun dial.

Make your own four-poster bed

You need a small cardboard box, four new pencils, colored paper, scraps of material, ribbons, scissors, sticky tape and glue.

1. Cut the box in half as shown. Cover both halves with colored paper.

Pencil tips upward

2. Cut neat crosses in the four corners of one of the halves. Push the pencils through the crosses.

3. Place the other half on the points of the pencils. Tape in place.

Tape inside

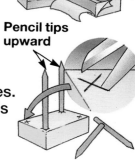

4. Glue strips of material to the top of the bed for curtains. Put two on each side.

Use material to cover the top of the bed.

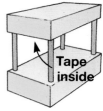

You could make pillows and blankets.

Tie with ribbons.

41

Homes in the Wild West

For many years, Indians had the West of America to themselves. 170 years ago, European settlers began to move there from the crowded East. At first they had to build their homes and grow their own food. Later, towns were built and people could buy things from shops.

Here is an early settler's home. It is built out of logs. Everything in it was made by the family or brought from the East.

Slots were cut to make the logs fit neatly together.

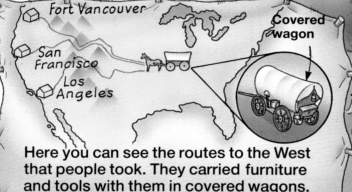

Fort Vancouver

San Francisco

Los Angeles

Covered wagon

Here you can see the routes to the West that people took. They carried furniture and tools with them in covered wagons.

Indian homes

The Indians moved around to follow herds of buffaloes which they killed for meat.

Teepees were often painted.

Home-made rocking chair

People shot wild animals and birds. They ate the meat.

They lived in tents made of animal skin. These were called teepees. They folded them up and took them along when they moved.

Woman packing up teepee.

They used feathers to stuff pillows and quilts.

This man is cutting down trees so he can build a barn.

The Bible was the only book in most homes.

THE BIBLE

Earth houses

Houses like this were known as soddies. Some are still lived in today.

Some parts of the West, such as Nebraska, had few trees. People who settled there built houses with lumps of earth cut out of the ground.

People kept rifles handy in case they were attacked by Indians or wild animals.

Hen house

Vegetable garden

People brought animals with them, although many died on the long journey.

Make a model teepee

You will need: stiff paper, clay, three straws, and a rubber band. pencil, large plate, scissors, sticky tape

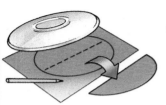

Corners

Tape

Leave bottom open for door.

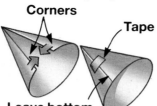

Line drawn around teepee on paper.

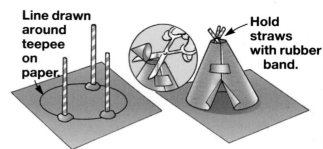

Hold straws with rubber band.

Draw around the plate on the paper. Cut out the circle. Fold it in half, then cut along the fold.

Take a half circle and pull the two corners together to make a cone. Tape across the join.

Draw around the teepee. Put 3 blobs of clay in the circle. Stick a straw in each.

Snip the top off the teepee. Pull the ends of the straws together and slide the teepee over them.

43

Terraced houses

About 150 years ago, many people moved to the towns. They came from the country to work in factories. They needed new houses.

Most were built joined in rows. These were called terraced houses. Lots could be fitted on to a small piece of land.

These terraced houses were built for factory workers.

Families were crowded inside. Many had to live in only one room.

Factory chimneys

Most rooms had a fireplace. People burned coal there for cooking and warmth. ▼

Chimney pots let smoke out from fireplaces.

Smoke from fires and factories made the houses dirty.

People fetched water from a pump in the street.

Doing the washing

Before gadgets such as washing machines were invented, housework was very tiring. Here you can see how a servant did the washing.

1. The servant heated water in a big pan, and poured it into a tub.

2. She used a stick called a dolly to beat the washing up and down inside the tub.

3. Next she scrubbed out any stains on a ridged scrubbing board.

4. Then she squeezed out the water with a rolling machine called a mangle.

5. Finally she took the washing outside and hung it on a line to dry.

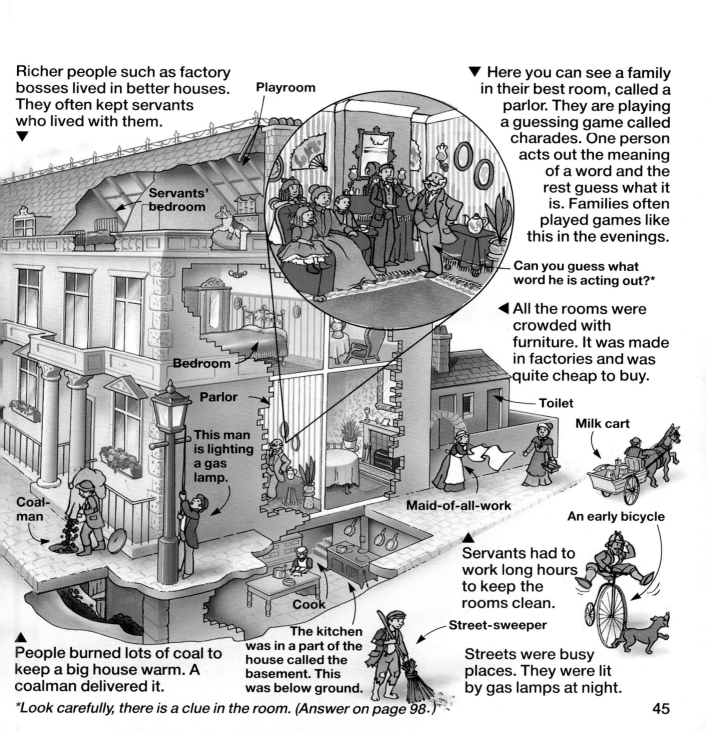

Richer people such as factory bosses lived in better houses. They often kept servants who lived with them.
▼

Playroom

Servants' bedroom

▼ Here you can see a family in their best room, called a parlor. They are playing a guessing game called charades. One person acts out the meaning of a word and the rest guess what it is. Families often played games like this in the evenings.

Can you guess what word he is acting out?*

Bedroom

◄ All the rooms were crowded with furniture. It was made in factories and was quite cheap to buy.

Parlor

This man is lighting a gas lamp.

Toilet

Milk cart

Coal-man

Maid-of-all-work

An early bicycle

▲ Servants had to work long hours to keep the rooms clean.

Cook

Street-sweeper

The kitchen was in a part of the house called the basement. This was below ground.

▲ People burned lots of coal to keep a big house warm. A coalman delivered it.

Streets were busy places. They were lit by gas lamps at night.

Look carefully, there is a clue in the room. (Answer on page 98.)

Other types of houses

In the 1930s, people built many sorts of houses. They made them convenient and healthy to live in. They gave them lots of windows, water taps and electricity.

Families used all sorts of new gadgets inside these homes. Some were used to help with the housework. Others were just for fun.

This American house had huge glass windows which let in lots of light. It also had a shady porch where people could sit in hot weather.

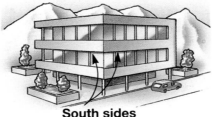

South sides

These apartments were built in Switzerland. The balconies and sitting room windows were all on the south sides so they got plenty of sun.

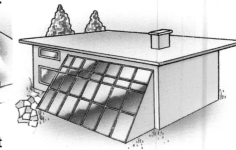

This Swedish house had a garden inside. Its glass wall let in enough light for the plants to grow.

Things people used

Here you can see some gadgets people used in their homes in the 1930s.

Electric lights were much brighter than ◀ candles or gas.

Vacuum cleaners helped people clean their houses thoroughly. ▶

The first vacuum cleaner was invented in 1899.

Refrigerators kept ▶ food fresh. This meant people did not have to buy it every day.

Gas and electric stoves ▲ were cleaner and safer than cooking over a fire.

This machine heated water, washed clothes and squeezed water out of them.

Electric boilers ▶ heated washing water quickly. Rich people even had washing machines. ◀

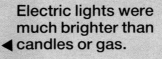

Boilers just heated water.

This record player was called a gramophone. It had to be wound up before it would play. ▶

Handle

Build a model house

Imagine a house you would like to live in. Try making a model of it. Below are some ideas to start you off.

You can cut out doors and windows if you like*. Make them any shape.

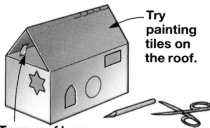

Try painting tiles on the roof.

Tape roof here

These British houses each had a garden. This helped stop people feeling over-crowded even though their houses were close together.

Many people were poorly paid or had no work. They had to live in old houses with no electricity or taps. Many were falling to pieces.

You could use a box for the main part. Paint it and add doors and windows. Fold a piece of thin card and tape it on to make a sloping roof.

Empty dishwashing liquid bottle as a tower

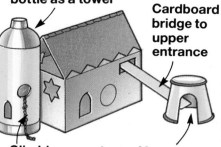

Cardboard bridge to upper entrance

Climbing rope to tower bedroom

Yogurt pot entrance

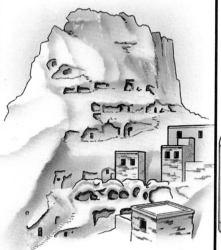
Not everybody wanted new homes. Some people in Turkey had always made their homes in caves. They were very comfortable and did not want to move.

Think of other things you could add to make a more interesting house like the one shown above.

*Get an adult to help you cut stiff cardboard and plastic. 47

Facts about homes

Earliest shelters

★The earliest known shelters were made about two million years ago. Their remains are in Tanzania, Africa.

Earliest castle

★The earliest castle is at Gomdan in the Yemen. It is over 1,900 years old and originally had 20 stories.

Expensive palace

★The grand Palace of Versailles was completed in 1682 for King Louis XIV of France. It was so expensive that he destroyed all records of payments to stop people finding out how much he spent.

Largest palace

★The largest palace in the world is the Imperial Palace in Peking, China. It covers an area of 177 acres. That is the same amount of space as 96 football fields joined together.

Forgotten city

★In A.D.79 Pompeii, a Roman city, was buried in stones and ashes from an erupting volcano. When archaeologist, Giuseppe Fiorelli uncovered it in 1861, he found streets and houses which had been untouched for hundreds of years.

Largest house

★The largest private house in the world is Biltmore House in the USA. It was built between 1890 and 1895 and has 250 rooms.

Highest home

★The highest home is 21,780 feet above sea-level, on a mountain in South America. It was built about 500 years ago.

Expensive furniture

★The highest price ever paid for a piece of furniture is two and three quarter million dollars. This was for an armchair which originally belonged to an American general, John Cadwalader.

Enormous bed

★The largest bed ever was made in 1430. It belonged to the Duke of Burgundy and was 12 feet wide and 19 feet long.

Earliest carpet

★The earliest carpet ever found is about 2,500 years old. It is now preserved in Leningrad, Russia.

Bright idea

★The electric lamp was invented by Thomas Edison in 1879.

FOOD AND EATING

Consultant: Shirley Bond S.R.D.

Contents

50   The first food

52   Ancient Egyptian food

54   Roman food

56   What the Vikings ate

58   Medieval food

60   Medieval banquets

62   Discovering different foods

64   Food in the New World

66   Better food in Europe

68   Kitchen inventions

70   Changes everywhere

72   Food facts and dates

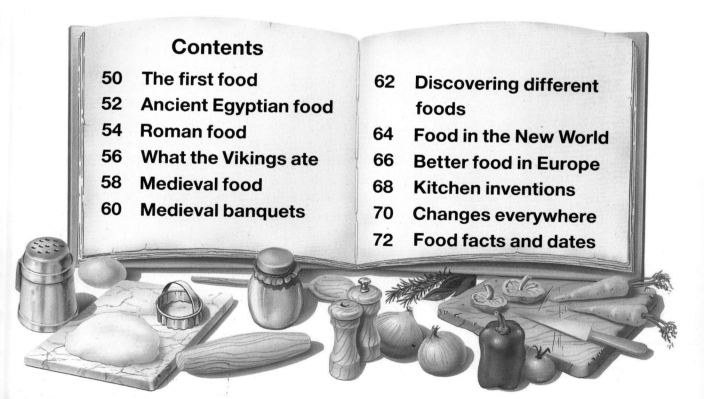

The first food

The first people spent a lot of time hunting animals and gathering food.

Bison

The men did the hunting. They killed animals such as deer, bison, horses, boar and mammoths with wood and stone weapons.

Stone tool

If the animal was big, they chopped it up near to where they killed it. Then they carried the pieces back to their camps.

They also caught fish from rivers and lakes. The very first people ate their food raw because they had not learned to make fire.

Digging stick

Women collected foods such as berries, bulbs, roots, mushrooms and nuts. They also gathered grubs, eggs and snails.

Learning to cook

People probably first found out that meat tasted better cooked when they dropped it in the fire by mistake. After that they cooked meat on sticks or on flat stones heated up by the fire.

The water was heated up with hot stones.

Hot stones

▲ Before cooking pots were invented, food was boiled in a pit. The pit was lined with skins and filled with water.

The first farmers

About 10,000 years ago, people noticed that when seeds were dropped on the ground they grew into plants.

Soon they began to dig the ground especially to plant seeds. These people were the first farmers.

The farmers also began to tame sheep, goats, dogs, pigs and cattle.▼

With these crops and animals, people now had grain, meat and milk. They hunted less as they had more food around them.

Hunting tricks

Hunters used tricks to help them catch animals. Here are some of them.

Disguise
They wore skins so that they could creep up on animals.

Traps

A bison falling into a pit dug by hunters.

They dug deep pits and covered them with sticks. The sticks broke when an animal stepped on them so it fell into the pit.

Fire

They chased animals with burning branches to drive them into swamps and over cliffs.

Animals were afraid of fire and ran away from it.

Sickle

River

They cut the crops with a tool called a sickle made from stone and wood.

Oven for bread

They built houses together near rivers. These were the first villages.

◀ Soon people learned to make cooking pots from clay, weave wool into clothes and make baskets.

◀ By grinding grain they made flour for bread. They baked the bread in dried mud ovens.

Some of these methods are still used in parts of the world.

51

Ancient Egyptian food

The Ancient Egyptians used the flood water from the River Nile to grow their crops. They could usually store enough of this water to last the whole year.

The river flooded every July and soaked the hard ground. The Egyptians dug channels to take the water to the fields.

Channel

Wheat was planted in October. By April it was ready to be cut. ▼

The wheat was cut using a sickle with a flint blade.

Sickle

Men put the wheat in baskets.

Cattle trampled on the wheat to separate the stalks from the grain.

Making bread

This is how the Egyptians made bread. They baked over 40 different kinds.

◄ The grain was ground to make flour.

Flour, water ▶ and salt were mixed to make dough.

◄ Fruit, nuts, garlic or honey might be added.

The dough ▶ was made into loaves and baked.

Oven

Women tossed the grain in the air. This removed its outside covering (chaff).

◄ Grain was stored in granaries. It was used to make bread, beer and cakes.

A scribe counted the baskets.

Grain was poured in here.

Granary

Workers had beer, bread, cheese and onions for lunch. Bread and beer were the main food and drink. ▶

Fishing

Egyptians ate a lot of fish from the Nile such as perch, mullet and eels.

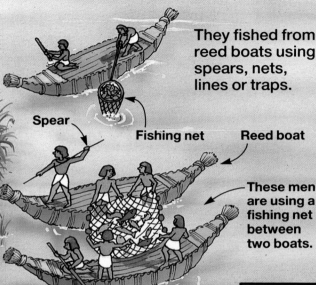

They fished from reed boats using spears, nets, lines or traps.

Spear

Fishing net

Reed boat

These men are using a fishing net between two boats.

Some fish were eaten fresh. Some were dried in the sun or put in jars with salt or oil to stop them going bad.

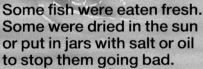

Hunting wild ducks with a throwing stick.

Bow and arrow

◄ They also hunted wild birds such as geese, ducks and storks. They hunted for sport as well as for food.

Tombs

The pictures and writing on the walls of Ancient Egyptian tombs tell us a lot about what they ate. They show people farming, shopping, cooking, baking and eating.

The Egyptians believed people had another life after they were dead. They put food and other useful things in a tomb when a person was buried. These were for the person to use in his next life.

Egyptian meals

Rich Egyptians ate many of the same things that we can buy today. Here are some of them.

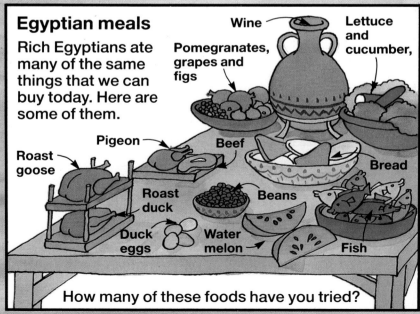

Wine

Lettuce and cucumber,

Pomegranates, grapes and figs

Pigeon

Beef

Bread

Roast goose

Roast duck

Beans

Duck eggs

Water melon

Fish

How many of these foods have you tried?

Roman food

The Romans came from Italy. The poor people who lived there ate mostly bread and a kind of porridge made from wheat.

Only rich people could afford meat, fish, cheese and vegetables. They ate very well and often had big dinner parties.

Preparing for a party

In rich houses, slaves spent all day preparing the food. Kitchens were hot and smoky because food was cooked on open fires.

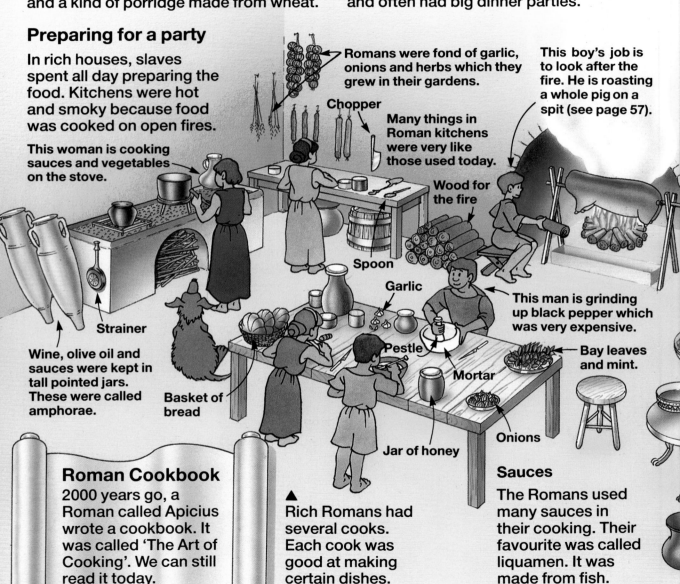

This woman is cooking sauces and vegetables on the stove.

Romans were fond of garlic, onions and herbs which they grew in their gardens.

Chopper

Many things in Roman kitchens were very like those used today.

This boy's job is to look after the fire. He is roasting a whole pig on a spit (see page 57).

Wood for the fire

Spoon

Garlic

This man is grinding up black pepper which was very expensive.

Strainer

Wine, olive oil and sauces were kept in tall pointed jars. These were called amphorae.

Basket of bread

Pestle

Mortar

Bay leaves and mint.

Jar of honey

Onions

Roman Cookbook

2000 years go, a Roman called Apicius wrote a cookbook. It was called 'The Art of Cooking'. We can still read it today.

▲ Rich Romans had several cooks. Each cook was good at making certain dishes.

Sauces

The Romans used many sauces in their cooking. Their favourite was called liquamen. It was made from fish.

A Roman recipe

This is how you can make a Roman bread pudding.

You will need:
1½ thick slices of bread,
300 ml (½ pint) milk,
150 ml (¼ pint) olive oil,
Honey

1. Cut the ▶ bread into fairly large pieces

◀ 2. Soak the pieces in the milk.

3. Fry them in hot oil.* Drain on paper towels. Serve with honey.

Good manners

After eating, it was polite to burp to show you had enjoyed the meal. Guests often brought napkins to take home filled with food to eat later.

*Get an adult to help you with this.

A dinner party

Parties started late in the afternoon and lasted many hours. Slaves brought the food from the kitchen.

Romans drank wine mixed with water. Sometimes honey was also added.

There were three couches in the dining room arranged around the table. People ate lying down.

People ate with their fingers. Sometimes they used spoons. There were no forks.

Red mullet

Lobster

Roast peacock

Chicken

Bread

Boar's head

Bowl of water

▲ There were three courses for a dinner. These people are eating a main course.

Guests washed their fingers after each course.

First course

Eggs

Stuffed dormice

Bread

Oysters and mushrooms

Salad

Snails

Dessert

Honey cakes

Stuffed dates

Nuts

Fruit

Fruit tarts

What the Vikings ate

The Vikings came from Sweden, Denmark and Norway. The weather there was cold and snowy in winter and the summers were short. Viking farmers had to work very hard to grow and store enough food to last through the long winter.

They grew barley, wheat, oats and rye to make into bread, porridge and beer.

In their small vegetable gardens they grew peas, onions and cabbages.

Cows, chickens, sheep, pigs and geese were kept for meat, milk and eggs.

The Vikings caught a lot of fish and hunted seals with spears.

They also caught sea-birds with nets and collected their eggs to eat.

Viking hunters killed wild animals such as boar and deer with bows and arrows.

Keeping food

The Vikings salted or dried a lot of meat and fish. This stopped it from going bad.

Meat was ▶ dried above a fire. Fish were dried in the sun.

Cutting up meat

◀ Pieces of meat were put in barrels with salt made from seawater.

Salt

Bread made from rye flour and oatcakes were baked on hot stones by the fire. ▶

Bread

Drinking cup made from cow horn

Beer

56

Viking meals

Vikings had two main meals a day at about eight in the morning and seven in the evening. They cooked, ate and slept in the one large room of their houses.

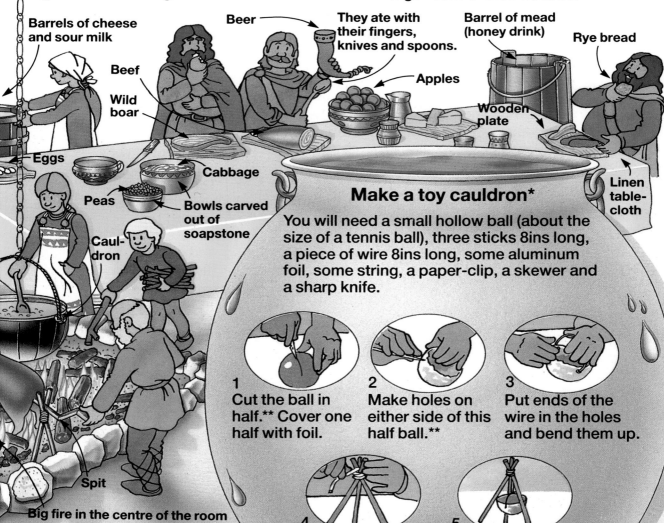

Barrels of cheese and sour milk

Beer

They ate with their fingers, knives and spoons.

Barrel of mead (honey drink)

Rye bread

Beef

Wild boar

Apples

Wooden plate

Eggs

Cabbage

Linen table-cloth

Peas

Bowls carved out of soapstone

Caul-dron

Make a toy cauldron*

You will need a small hollow ball (about the size of a tennis ball), three sticks 8ins long, a piece of wire 8ins long, some aluminum foil, some string, a paper-clip, a skewer and a sharp knife.

1 Cut the ball in half.** Cover one half with foil.

2 Make holes on either side of this half ball.**

3 Put ends of the wire in the holes and bend them up.

4 Tie the sticks with the string to make a tripod.

5 Hook the cauldron to the string with the paper-clip.

Spit

Big fire in the centre of the room

Food was cooked on iron poles called spits or in large metal pots called cauldrons over a fire.

*DO NOT try to light a fire under your cauldron.
** Get an adult to help you.

57

Medieval food

In Medieval times, many people in Europe were poor farmers. They lived in small villages belonging to a lord. They had to work very hard for the lord and ate the same food almost every day.

Life in a village

Each village had three big fields. Every family had strips of land in each field. There they grew wheat and rye for bread, barley for beer, and oats.

They also kept animals for milk, meat and eggs and grew vegetables in small vegetable gardens.

Pigs

Pork and bacon from pigs was the main meat for villagers. Most families kept a pig.

Pigs were also kept in towns. They often wandered around the streets and got in the way.

Apple tree

Deer

Chickens

Pear tree

Garden for cabbages, herbs, leeks, peas, onions and beans.

Well

Lord's house

Pond

They caught fish and eels ▶ from ponds and rivers. A lot were salted and dried for the winter.

Bees for honey

Church

Each year one of the fields was left resting with nothing planted in it. This helped the soil get back its goodness.

They had to ▶ pay to have grain ground into flour at the lord's water mill. They paid again to bake bread in his oven.

Water mill

As there was no food for animals in winter, most were killed in the autumn. Meat was smoked or salted to stop it going bad.

Sheep ▶

Meals

For breakfast villagers had bread and watery beer (ale). Beer was their usual drink. For lunch they had the same, maybe with cheese and an onion.

In the evening they had thick soup (pottage) made from things such as pork, onions, cabbage, beans, oats and water.

Soup was made in a pot above the fire. The pot was emptied out only once a year before Lent (see Church days).

Each day more food was added to the leftovers.

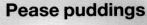

Pease puddings

Dumplings were also cooked inside the pot. Some were made from rye flour, others from dried peas and beans. These were called pease puddings. They were tied in a cloth and hung in the pot.

Church days

It was a Christian church rule that nobody must eat meat on Fridays or in Lent (40 days before Easter). During this time they ate a lot of salted fish.

The only time they ate well and did not work was on Christmas Day and a few other holidays.

Dancing on May Day.

Food around the world

These are some of the things people ate at this time around the world.

Bread, cabbage, beans, salted pork, cheese, soup.

Rice, pork, vegetables.

Corn, deer, beans, fish, bison, turkey.

Corn pancakes, tomatoes, potatoes, peppers, beans.

Millet porridge, beans, milk, beef.

Rice, vegetables and a spicy sauce.

North America

Europe

India China

Africa

South America

Australia

N

Medieval banquets

In Medieval times rich families lived in big houses or castles. They had cooks to make many different kinds of food. They often invited guests to a banquet.

Banquet Menu

These are some of the many dishes guests had to choose from:

First Course
Eggs in cream sauce
Whole baby pig
Eel pie

Second Course
Roast deer, ox, chicken, goose, peacock and swan
Boar's head
Lampreys (kind of fish)

Third Course
Meat pies
Frumenty (wheat with eggs, stock and milk)
Liver dumplings

Dessert
Pear tart / Cherry pudding

Ale, Mead, Wine

Banquets started in the evening. The lord's family and most important guests sat at a raised table (the high table) facing the room. They were given a spoon and napkin. Other guests brought their own.

Important guests had a servant to taste their food to make sure it wasn't poisoned. ▼

Instead of plates, people had thick, square slices of bread called trenchers. ▼

Lord

Taster

Salt cellar

High table

Trencher

People used small knives which they carried with them.

A lot of spices, herbs and garlic were used to flavor food.

Rich people often went hunting and brought back pheasants, deer and wild boar to eat.

Jester

People ate mostly with their fingers. They washed their hands between courses. ▶

They threw ▶ scraps of food and bones on the floor for the dogs.

Bones for the dogs

Bowls of mustard and spices

Musicians played for the guests while they were eating.

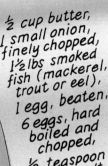

◀ Sometimes a cook roasted a peacock or swan. He sewed its feathers and skin back on before it was served.

Small birds

Salted fish

Fish pasties

Most guests shared a dish of food with another guest. ▼

How to make Medieval fish pasties

You will need:

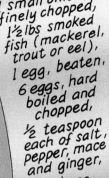

½ cup butter,
1 small onion, finely chopped,
1½ lbs smoked fish (mackerel, trout or eel),
1 egg, beaten,
6 eggs, hard boiled and chopped,
½ teaspoon each of salt, pepper, mace and ginger,
1 package pie crust.

1
Set oven to Gas Mark 4*. In a pan, fry the onion in the butter.

2
Remove bones from fish. Flake it with fork. Add onion.

3
Add spices, pepper, salt and chopped eggs. Roll out pastry.

4
Cut out 4in circles. Put some mixture in the middle of each one.

5
Wet edges of circles with water. Fold pastry over. Pinch edges.

6
Put on oiled baking tray. Brush with egg. Bake for 25 minutes.

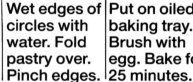

Surprise pies

A cook sometimes made a big empty pie. As a joke, after it was cooked, he put small live birds into the pie through a hole in the bottom. When the pie was cut, the birds flew out, surprising the guests.

Can you see a surprise pie in the main picture?

Discovering different foods

About 500 years ago, European sailors began to explore the world. They found many countries which they had not known about before. They also found a lot of new foods. They brought some of these back to Europe.

New foods for Europe

These are some of the new foods that travellers brought to Europe.

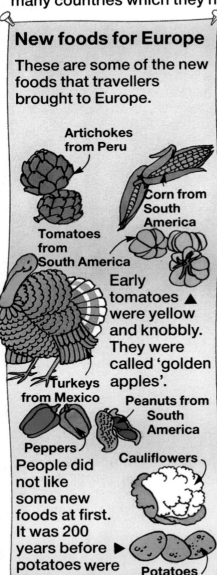

Artichokes from Peru

Corn from South America

Tomatoes from South America

Early tomatoes were yellow and knobbly. They were called 'golden apples'.

Turkeys from Mexico

Peanuts from South America

Peppers

Cauliflowers

People did not like some new foods at first. It was 200 years before potatoes were very popular.

Potatoes from Peru

The search for spices

Cinnamon

Pepper

Ginger

Nutmeg

At this time, a lot of spices were used to flavor food, especially meat that was going bad.

These spices were brought to Europe across land by Arab traders. They were very expensive.

As they sailed, they found countries such as North and South America. They called them the New World.

India

Sri Lanka

East Indies

The spices came from countries in the East, such as India, the East Indies and Sri Lanka.

The European sailors began to look for a way to the East to bring back the spices by sea.

They often just took what they wanted and treated the people living there very badly or killed them.

In the kitchen

Cooking was still done over an open fire. In a rich home they ate a lot of meat. This was cooked on a spit. Bread and pies were cooked in a separate oven.

Sailors' food

Sailors spent weeks at sea. They had little fresh water and no way of storing fresh food. The food they took often went bad.

Dry cheese

Bread oven

Metal cauldrons hanging above the fire were used for cooking soups and stews.

Smoked meats

Pans to catch fat

Biscuits (often full of worms)

Salted fish and meat

Beer

They sometimes ate sea-birds, sharks and rats.

Scurvy

Many sailors died of a disease called scurvy. This was because they had no fresh fruit or vegetables.

Sugar was sold in lumps. It was cut up with sugar cutters.

Sugar cutters

Sugar

Store cupboard

Jug of beer

Spice box

Basket of vegetables

The rich had metal plates. Others had wooden ones.

Aztec food

North America

Mexico is in Central America.

South America

The Aztec people lived in Mexico. In 1521, Spanish sailors came seeking gold. They conquered the Aztecs.

The sailors had never seen many of these foods before.

Aztecs ate corn porridge and pancakes (tortillas), tomatoes, peppers, beans, turkey and chocolate.

The sailors liked some Aztec foods and brought them back to Europe.

The Aztecs also ate dogs and sometimes frogs, tadpoles, newts, worms, flies, ants, and lizards.

Food in the New World

People from Europe began to travel to the New World (North and South America) to start new lives there.

The story of Thanksgiving

In 1620, a group of people sailed from England to the east coast of America. They landed on 10th November.

It was too late in the year and too cold to plant the rye and wheat seeds they had brought with them.

The Indians who lived there gave them food. Even so, only half the English people survived the hard winter.

In the spring, the Indians taught them how to grow corn and beans and to hunt. Their next harvest was good.

Corn flour bread

They made a feast of turkey and other foods to celebrate. They invited the Indians who had helped them.

Americans still celebrate this harvest on Thanksgiving day. They have a meal of turkey and pumpkin pie.

Pumpkin pie

You will need:

¼ cup butter,
2 lbs pumpkin, peeled and sliced,
3 apples, peeled, cored and sliced,
½ lb sultanas,
1 lb pie dough,
3 eggs, beaten,
1 cup cream,
1 cup brown sugar,
½ teaspoon each of ground ginger, cinnamon, nutmeg, cloves and allspice.

1 Fry the pumpkin in the butter on a low heat until light brown. Keep the juice that is made.

2 Put the pumpkin pieces into a bowl over a pan of boiling water. Cook until just soft.

This is how pumpkin pie was made over 300 years ago.

3

In another pan, stew the apples and sultanas in the pumpkin juice until they are just soft.

4

Roll out the pastry and line a 9in flan dish. Put a layer of apples and sultanas in it.

5

Add the beaten eggs to the pumpkin. Mix in the cream, sugar and spices. Pour into the flan dish.

6

Cook the pie at Gas Mark 6* for 10 minutes, then at Mark 4** for 20-25 minutes. Serve hot.

New drinks in Europe

390 years ago tea, coffee and chocolate were brought to Europe for the first time. Coffee houses opened where people could buy these new drinks and talk to their friends.

In many cities in Europe, such as Paris and Vienna, a lot of coffee houses later became cafés.

Chocolate

Chocolate was brought to Europe from South America and the West Indies. At first it was always made into a drink, no one ate it. ▶

China cup

Tea

Tea has been drunk in China for about 1,300 years. It was first brought to Europe in 1610.

Tea soon became a popular drink, especially in England. ▶

Coffee

Coffee first grew in Africa. It was later brought to Europe from Turkey. ▶

A coffee house

Samuel Pepys

Samuel Pepys lived in London over 300 years ago. He wrote a diary which tells us about the food he ate. This is what he gave his guests for dinner in 1663.

Rabbit and chicken stew
A leg of mutton
Three carps (fish)
A side of lamb
A dish of roasted pigeons
Four lobsters
Three tarts
Lamprey (fish) pie
A dish of anchovies
Good wine

*Electric 400°F or 200°C.   **Electric 350°F or 180°C.

Better food in Europe

About 230 years ago farmers began to look for new ways of growing food and breeding animals to eat.

This meant that the rich people had better food. Poor people still had very little choice of food.

A meal in a town house

Rich families, like this one, ate their main meal at about six or seven o'clock in the evening.

Poor people often had to beg for food.

Sugar

Sugar came from large farms, called sugar plantations, in places such as South America and the West Indies. People from Africa were captured and forced to work as slaves on the farms.

Table manners

In 1788, an English book called 'The Honours of the Table' told guests how to behave while they were eating. It said you must not:

◀ Scratch any part of your body or pick your teeth.

◀ Blow your nose or spit, or sit too far from the table.

If you needed to go to the rest room, you were supposed to creep out without anybody noticing. When you came back, you could not say where you had been.

Because sugar ▶ was much cheaper than before, there were many different kinds of sweet cakes and puddings.

Forks

400 years ago people began using forks in Italy. Over the following 100 years, forks started to be used in the rest of Europe.

Early forks only had two prongs.

Fork with three prongs from 200 years ago

People began to eat fruit raw instead of always cooked.

Gardens

Gardeners had better seeds, so they began to grow better kinds of fruit and vegetables.

The first sandwich

One day in 1760, John Montague, Earl of Sandwich played cards for 24 hours non-stop.

He asked for his meat to be put between two pieces of bread so that he could eat and carry on playing. This was the first sandwich.

◀ Rich people had beautiful plates and dishes made of china or silver.

Meat

Farmers had new foods which kept animals alive over the winter, so there was more fresh meat.

Potato pie

Potatoes were now used in many different recipes. This potato pie makes a lunch for six people.

You will need:

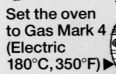

3 lbs potatoes, peeled or scrubbed,
2 large carrots, finely grated,
Juice of 2 oranges,
½ cup butter
2 eggs,
1 teaspoon sugar,
Salt and pepper,
1 cup grated cheese

1 Set the oven to Gas Mark 4 (Electric 180°C, 350°F) ▶

2 Boil the potatoes until soft. ◀ Mash them.

3 Add all other ingredients. Beat them into potato. ▶

4 Put mixture into a dish. Bake for 20 minutes. ◀ Serve hot.

Eating too much

Rich men often ate too much meat and too many cakes, pies and sweet things. They also drank far too much alcohol.

They often got a painful disease called gout. This made their fingers and toes swell up.

French cooks

About 300 years ago French cooks first became famous for their good cooking.

Cooks wrote recipe books which became very popular.

The most famous cook was Antoinin Carême. He was called 'the cook of kings and the king of cooks'.

Ships

Different countries around the world grew different kinds of food. Many of these were brought to Europe in sailing ships.

Kitchen inventions

Inventions such as cooking ranges, gas ovens, ice boxes and cans made cooking and storing food much easier. For a long time, however, these things were too expensive for poor people to buy. They still ate simple food which they cooked over an open fire as they had done for thousands of years.

Canned food

In 1813, food was sealed in cans for the first time. To start with, cans were used mainly by sailors as the food kept for a long time. By 1880, cans were very popular.

A can from 1880

An early tin opener

Canned food could be sent all over the world. A lot was sent to Europe from Australia.

Factories

Some food was now made in factories by machines, instead of being made by hand at home.

Machine for mixing dough for bread from 1880

Cooking ranges

Some people could ▶ afford the new kind of ovens made from iron. These were called cooking ranges.

They were heated by a coal or wood fire. Many could heat hot water too.

Coal fire   Oven

The ashes had to be cleaned from the grate every day.

Gas cookers

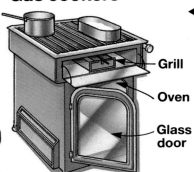

Grill

Oven

Glass door

◀ Gas cookers were invented in 1802, but most homes didn't have one for another 100 years.

Gas cookers were clean and easy to use but, like ranges, they didn't have a temperature control. You judged the heat of the oven by putting your hand inside.

Ice Boxes

You had to put a ▶ big block of ice inside the first ice boxes. This kept the food cold.

This wooden ice box was made in America in 1874.

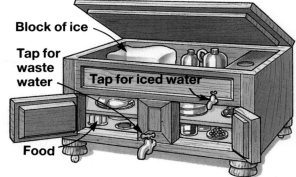

Block of ice

Tap for waste water

Tap for iced water

Food

Factory workers' food

The people who went to towns to work in factories had little money and poor food. The only hot meal many of them got was free soup from soup kitchens.

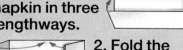
Soup kitchen in 1851

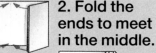

A factory worker's day.
5 a.m. Get up.
6-8 a.m. Work.
Breakfast - tea or coffee and bread.
Back to work until 12pm
Lunch - potatoes with lard, sometimes a little bacon.
1p.m. - 7p.m. work.
Supper - tea or beer, potatoes or porridge, bread, perhaps a little meat.

Potato disease

In 1845, potatoes all over Europe started rotting in the fields because of a disease called blight.

Potatoes were the main food for a lot of poor people.

Poor people starved because they had nothing else to eat. In Ireland, thousands died. Many left to go to other countries such as America.

Fold a party napkin

Try this with a large paper or linen napkin.

1. Fold the napkin in three lengthways.

2. Fold the ends to meet in the middle.

3. Fold down top corners and turn the napkin over.

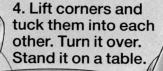

4. Lift corners and tuck them into each other. Turn it over. Stand it on a table.

Rich people's food

As always, rich people could afford many different kinds of food. They had servants to buy, cook and serve their meals. They often had dinner parties with seven or more courses.

A dinner party 100 years ago

Rich people had beautiful china and many kinds of knives, forks, spoons and glasses.

Changes everywhere

The way food is grown, prepared, sold, cooked and eaten has changed a lot in the last 100 years. Electricity, for example, has made a big difference on farms and in factories as well as in kitchens.

The first electric cooker was made in 1895, but to start with most people could not afford new electrical things. Below you can see some of the things people with enough money could buy by about 1930.

Shopping

Until about 40 years ago there were no supermarkets. People had to go to several shops to buy different things. Food was not usually sold in packages. The shopkeeper weighed and packed the amount you wanted.

1930s Electric kitchen

Early dishwashers looked like this. The first was made in 1899. ▼

A few homes now had electric ice boxes to keep food fresh.

Dishwasher

Electric kettle

Refrigerator

Some kinds of food were sold in packages.

Electric and gas cookers were cleaner and safer than fires. The first cooker with a temperature control was made in 1933.

Pickled onions

Dried raisins

Rationing

During the Second World War (1939-1945) food was short, so in some countries it was rationed. This meant each person could only have a small amount of certain foods each week.

9oz sugar

2oz coffee

47½oz milk

1½oz jam

A little meat

3½oz cheese

½ egg

9oz fat

A ration book showed what each person could have.

RATION BOOK

People still ▶ smoked, dried or pickled food to stop it going bad.

Smoked fish

More food could now be bought in cans.

Using machines

In the past people grew all their own food and did everything by hand. Now most food comes from large farms. It is often prepared and put in packages by machines. This, for example, is how bread is made from wheat today.

Wheat is ▶ grown on a farm and cut down by a machine called a combine harvester.

Combine harvester

The wheat is ▶ ground into flour by machines in a big factory.

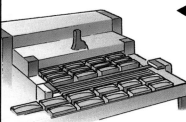

◀ Bread is baked, sliced and packed in a bakery. This oven bakes 2,400 loaves an hour.

Look at page 52 to see how Ancient Egyptians made bread 5000 years ago.

Early electric toasters had to be plugged into a cooker. The first was made in 1909.

Toaster

Bread

Sliced bread could be bought by 1930, but most people cut up their bread at home.

Restaurants

The idea of eating out started in France in 1765. Restaurants have only become popular in other places in the last 100 years.

Many modern restaurants serve food from other countries.

At take-out restaurants you can buy meals to take home.

No change

Some people in the world still hunt, fish and gather food or grow the food they need.

People in the Kalahari desert in Botswana use bows and arrows for hunting.

Many people in the world still don't get enough to eat. Some aid groups try to help by looking for better ways to grow and share food.

Food facts and dates

Ancient chopsticks

★Chinese people have used chopsticks for 3,500 years and still eat with them today.

Whistling for your supper

★In Medieval times, monks were not allowed to talk during meals. They solved the problem of asking for things by using sign language and whistling. They had more than 100 different signs, and even used their feet.

Below the salt

★Salt was very expensive during Medieval times. Only people at the high table (see page 60) had a salt-cellar, or bowl for salt. People at other tables were said to be "below the salt". This showed that they were less important.

Hot, hot chocolate

★In about 1630, some people in Spain liked to add hot-tasting pods of chilli peppers to their recipes for hot chocolate drinks.

Farming news

★One of the earliest books telling people how to grow food comes from Sumer. It was written in about the year 2,500BC and was called the "Farmer's Almanac".

Flying fish?

★Many Medieval people believed that the barnacle goose was born in the sea and counted it as a fish.

Gadget "firsts"

★The first food mixer was made by the Hamilton Beach Company in 1910.

★The first pop-up toaster was designed by C. Strite in 1927.

A corny tale

★Maize (corn) has been grown in South America since about the year 2000BC. Remains of maize plants which are thought to be over 80,000 years old have been found in Mexico.

Wheat machine

★The first machine for cutting down wheat was invented in 1826. Before this, all crops had to be cut by hand, which was very slow.

Egyptian bread and beer

★Bread was such an important food to the Ancient Egyptians that workers were given some as part of their wages.

★Their beer had so many lumps in it that it was often strained through a pottery strainer before it was drank.

TRAVEL AND TRANSPORT

Consultant: Dr Michael Hitchcock

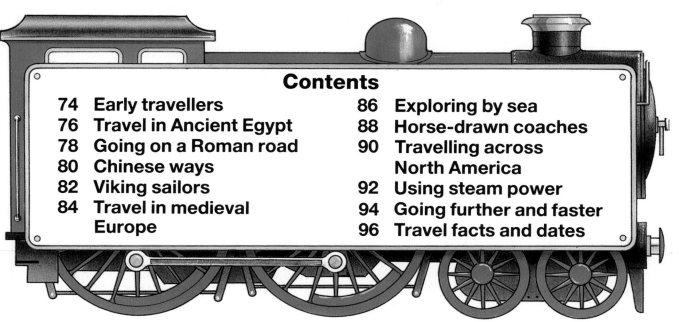

Contents

74 **Early travellers**
76 **Travel in Ancient Egypt**
78 **Going on a Roman road**
80 **Chinese ways**
82 **Viking sailors**
84 **Travel in medieval Europe**

86 **Exploring by sea**
88 **Horse-drawn coaches**
90 **Travelling across North America**
92 **Using steam power**
94 **Going further and faster**
96 **Travel facts and dates**

Language adviser: Betty Root M.B.E.

Early travellers

Long ago, people got food by hunting wild animals and picking nuts and berries. They walked from place to place to find their food.

They carried everything they owned with them, and camped in caves or shelters.

People had to watch out for dangerous animals.

Basket of spare clothes

They put things into baskets and bags to make them easier to carry.

People could drag baskets and bags on a frame made of branches.

Using animals

Later, people became farmers. They kept animals and grew plants for food. They used animals to help carry their harvest and other things.

They put loads on a wooden sled. They tied the sled to their animals and got them to pull it along.

Some farmers fixed round wooden shapes under the sledge to help it go more easily. These were the first wheels.

Their tools were made of stone. They were heavy.

Two could carry a heavy bag between them on a pole.

Making baskets and bags

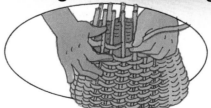

People made baskets by weaving bendy twigs together. Baskets are still made like this today.

They made bags by sewing animal skins together. They used long needles shaped out of bone.

Travelling over water

All over the world people made boats so they could cross water or travel swiftly down rivers and streams.

The simplest boats were ▶ logs tied together to make a raft. These were paddled along with branches.

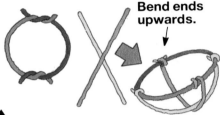

◀ Dug-outs were made by hollowing out logs. People lit a fire to burn out the center. Afterwards, they scraped out the burnt bits.

Some people tied bundles ▶ of reeds together to make a boat. Here you can see one kind used in South America.

◀ Others stretched skins over a round wooden frame. This made a boat called a coracle. They smeared tar over it to keep water out.

Near the North Pole, people ▶ used a narrow skin boat called a kayak. This was fast and easy to steer. Eskimos still use them today.

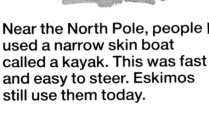

Make a model coracle

You need a plastic bag, pipe cleaners, scissors, stiff cardboard and sticky tape.

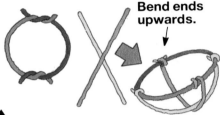

Bend ends upwards.

▲ Twist two pipe cleaners together to make a circle. Make two others into a cross. Fix the cross on to the circle as shown.

Frame

▲ Cut a sheet of plastic from the bag. Put it over the frame. Tape the edges down inside the coracle.

You could make pipe cleaner people to go inside.

▲ Cut a strip of cardboard. Tape it inside the coracle to make a seat. Float the finished coracle in a bowl of water.

Travel in Ancient Egypt

The Egyptians lived on the banks of the River Nile. The easiest way for them to travel was by boat along the river.

Trading boats

Wooden boats took grain, ropes and jewelry to Byblos and other towns near the Mediterranean Sea. They carried silver, oils and wood back up the Nile.

The wind blew against a huge sail and pushed the boat along. When the wind was blowing the wrong way, sailors took the sail down and rowed the boat.

Mediterranean Sea
Byblos
EGYPT
River Nile
North
W—E
S

This map shows Egypt.

Sailors used a weighted rope to check how deep the water was.

Trading boat with its sail up.

Front

Trading boat with its sail up.

Going north and south

The wind usually blew southwards along the Nile. Ships going south could use their sails while ships going north were rowed with their sails down.

Going north

Going south

Egyptians were so used to this that in their picture writing a ship with its sail up meant going south. A ship with its sail down meant going north.

The back of the boat was carved to look like an Egyptian flower called a lotus.

This man is using a paddle to move the boat along.

Hunting boats

Smaller boats were used for hunting water birds and fishing. They were made out of bundles of reeds tied together.

Cats were trained to help people hunt birds.

Hunting boat

Reeds hold a lot of air so they floated very well.

Sailors pushed these paddles into the water to steer the boat.

A travelling god

The Egyptians believed that the sun was a god called Ra. They thought he travelled in a magic boat that flew across the sky.

Sun god

Trading boat being rowed.

This thick rope helped to make the boat strong.

Front

Travel on land

The Nile flooded every year so its banks were often muddy. The rest of the land was sandy desert. It was difficult to travel over the mud and sand. Here are some of the ways Egyptians did it.

Donkeys

Traders loaded donkeys with baskets so they could take goods across the ▶ desert to swap or sell.

Oarsmen faced the back of the boat.

Travelling chairs

◀ Rich people got servants to carry them in travelling chairs called palanquins.

Palanquin

Each oarsman pulled an oar to make the boat go forward.

Sand sleds

People pulled heavy loads on sleds. Sometimes they put rollers underneath to help the sled slide more easily.

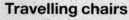

Rollers were moved to the front.

Faster travel

Chariot

3,700 years ago, the Hyksos people* invaded Egypt. They used chariots pulled by horses. The Egyptians were amazed by the speed of these chariots. Rich Egyptians began to use them for hunting and fighting.

*These were a tribe that came from Asia.

Going on a Roman road

The Romans came from Italy and conquered many lands in Europe and North Africa. They built over 48,000 miles of roads across them.

All sorts of people travelled across the lands. Everyone could go more easily on smooth Roman roads than over rough ground or paths.

Soldiers could march 18 miles in one day.

Soldiers marched to every land to keep order there.

Chariot races

In Rome and other cities, chariot races were held on race-tracks. Many people watched them. They used to bet on which driver would win.

Messengers rode non-stop on horses or in fast chariots.

Poor people walked. They could not afford to travel any other way.

Chariot

How the Romans built a road

Builders worked out the shortest route. They built the road along it like this:

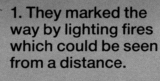

1. They marked the way by lighting fires which could be seen from a distance.

2. A trench was dug between the fires. It was at least 20 feet wide.

3. They packed the trench with layers of broken stones, gravel and sand.

4. They covered the top with large, flat stones called paving stones.

Crossing rivers

Some roads went through shallow rivers. People had to wade into the water. These crossing places were called fords.

Ford

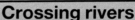

Roman bridges are called viaducts.

Romans built bridges over deep rivers. They made them by building strong arches out of brick or stone.

Arch

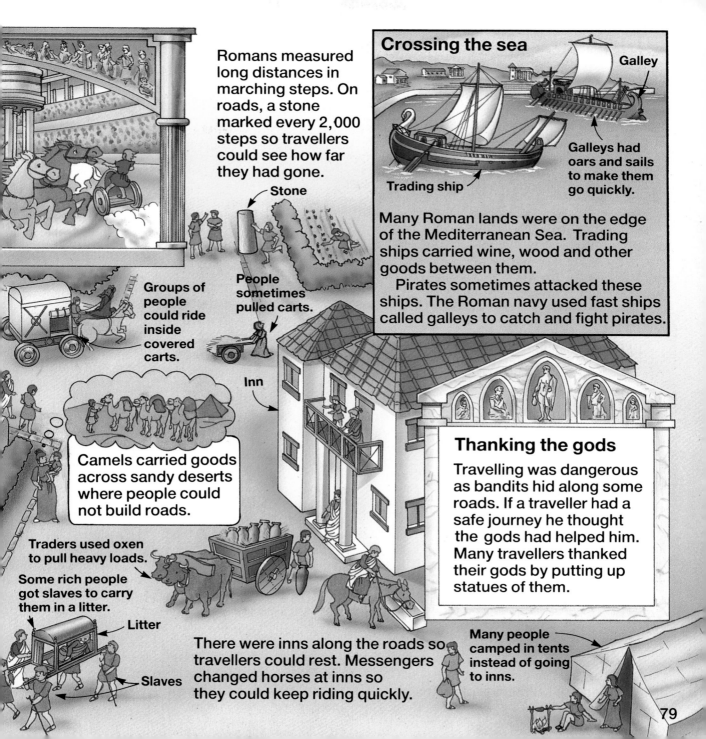

Romans measured long distances in marching steps. On roads, a stone marked every 2,000 steps so travellers could see how far they had gone.

Stone

People sometimes pulled carts.

Groups of people could ride inside covered carts.

Crossing the sea

Galley

Galleys had oars and sails to make them go quickly.

Trading ship

Many Roman lands were on the edge of the Mediterranean Sea. Trading ships carried wine, wood and other goods between them.

Pirates sometimes attacked these ships. The Roman navy used fast ships called galleys to catch and fight pirates.

Inn

Camels carried goods across sandy deserts where people could not build roads.

Traders used oxen to pull heavy loads.

Some rich people got slaves to carry them in a litter.

Litter

Slaves

Thanking the gods

Travelling was dangerous as bandits hid along some roads. If a traveller had a safe journey he thought the gods had helped him. Many travellers thanked their gods by putting up statues of them.

There were inns along the roads so travellers could rest. Messengers changed horses at inns so they could keep riding quickly.

Many people camped in tents instead of going to inns.

79

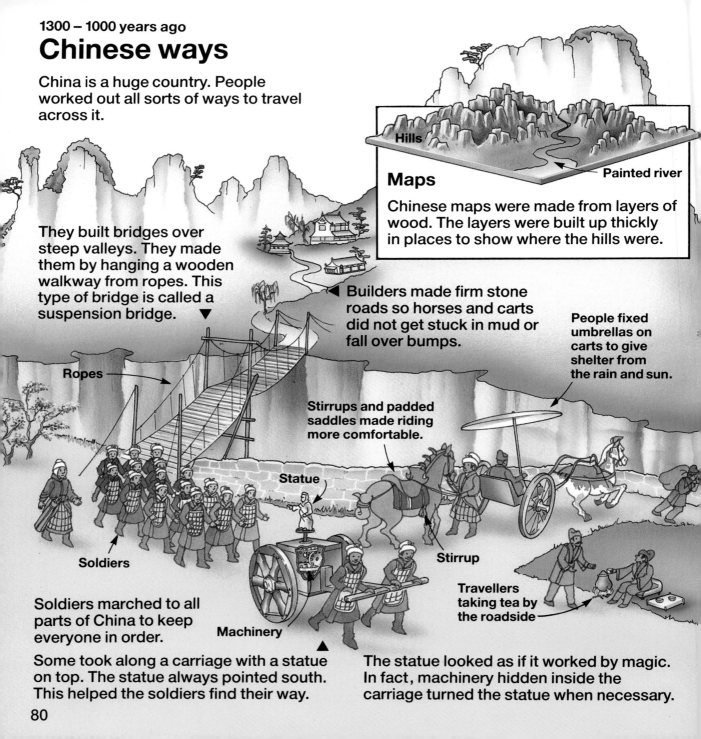

Chinese ways

China is a huge country. People worked out all sorts of ways to travel across it.

Hills

Painted river

Maps

Chinese maps were made from layers of wood. The layers were built up thickly in places to show where the hills were.

They built bridges over steep valleys. They made them by hanging a wooden walkway from ropes. This type of bridge is called a suspension bridge. ▼

◄ Builders made firm stone roads so horses and carts did not get stuck in mud or fall over bumps.

People fixed umbrellas on carts to give shelter from the rain and sun.

Ropes

Stirrups and padded saddles made riding more comfortable.

Statue

Soldiers

Stirrup

Machinery

Soldiers marched to all parts of China to keep everyone in order.

Some took along a carriage with a statue on top. The statue always pointed south. This helped the soldiers find their way.

Travellers taking tea by the roadside

The statue looked as if it worked by magic. In fact, machinery hidden inside the carriage turned the statue when necessary.

Moving home

Some people lived in felt tents on plains at the edges of China. They herded animals and had to move around to find grass for them. People like this who move around a lot are called nomads.

Tent packed on camel.

The Great Wall of China

The Chinese built a huge wall to keep enemies out of China. It was so big, people could travel on top of it.

Travelling by junk

Boats called junks carried people and goods along rivers. Some junks sailed across the sea to other countries such as India.

Junks like this one are still used in China today.

People put sails on wheelbarrows so the wind helped move heavy loads.

Some balanced awkward loads on poles so they could carry them easily.

Dangerous rivers

Some rivers were rocky and flowed so quickly that it was dangerous for junks to sail on them. Instead, people put on harnesses and pulled the junks along.

Sails had wooden strips inside to make them stiff.

People slept and ate under these covers.

The rudder was turned to the left or the right to steer the ship.

81

Viking sailors

The Vikings were brave sailors. They sailed along rivers and across seas to many European countries and to America.

This map shows the ▶ countries Viking sailors reached from their homelands in Sweden, Denmark and Norway.

Vikings often made trips to buy and sell goods. But sometimes they set out to attack and rob. Then they used boats with carved dragon heads. They hoped these would scare enemies.

Vikings used boats like this to make their surprise attacks.

The boat wasn't very deep. This was so it could sneak up shallow rivers.

Vikings made their boats from wooden planks. They were nailed on top of each other so they overlapped.

A flag showed the sailors which way the wind was blowing.

Carved dragon head

Viking robbers captured animals as well as treasure.

Sailors kept their belongings in chests.

At night sailors slept in skin sleeping bags.

Nails

Sheep's wool and tar were stuffed between planks to keep water out.

Sailors watched for certain birds and seaweeds. If they saw them they knew they were near land.

Norway
Sweden
Greenland
Russia
America
British Isles
Denmark
France
Istanbul
Spain
Italy
Mediterranean Sea
N W E S

Raven guides

A Viking called Floki Vilggerdarson used ravens to help him find land. He carried them on his ship and let them go one at a time.

If a raven flew off, Floki followed it. He knew it would fly to the nearest land. But if it returned quickly, he knew there was no land near.

The boat was steered with a broad paddle called a steerboard.

Travel on land

The Vikings were used to travelling in cold northern countries. They used skates, skis and sleds for crossing ice and snow.

Many sleds were pulled by horses. Vikings fitted spikes to the horses' hooves. This gave them a good grip on the ice.

Spike

Oars

◀ Vikings used oars to row boats along when there was no wind or they wanted to make a fast getaway.

Cover

Sailors pulled ropes to turn the sail so it caught the wind.

Oars went through holes in the side.

Sailors from Arabia

While Vikings were sailing around Europe, Arabs were sailing to East Africa, India and China. Arab sailors told strange stories about the places they found. These were written down in a book you can still read, called 'The Voyages of Sinbad the Sailor'.

These triangular sails caught more wind than the sail on a Viking boat.

An Arab ship

Travel in medieval Europe

People in Europe knew little about the rest of the world. Some travellers went a little way into Asia and Africa but most kept to the lands near the Mediterranean Sea.

The map shows a one-legged creature that was supposed to use its foot as a sun-shade.

◀ People had to guess what the world was like. They based picture maps like this on stories from the Bible as well as travellers' tales.

Australia and America aren't on the map as Europeans did not know about them.

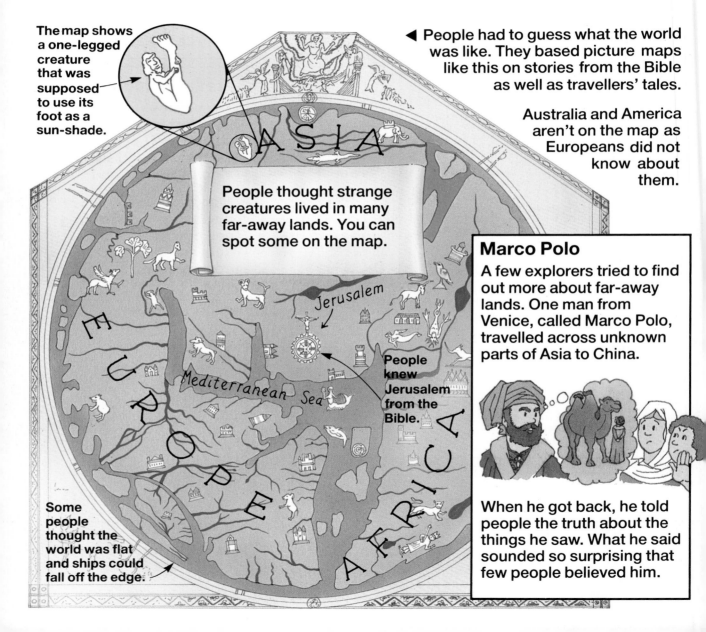

ASIA

People thought strange creatures lived in many far-away lands. You can spot some on the map.

Jerusalem

People knew Jerusalem from the Bible.

EUROPE

Mediterranean Sea

AFRICA

Some people thought the world was flat and ships could fall off the edge.

Marco Polo

A few explorers tried to find out more about far-away lands. One man from Venice, called Marco Polo, travelled across unknown parts of Asia to China.

When he got back, he told people the truth about the things he saw. What he said sounded so surprising that few people believed him.

Buying bones

Pilgrims (see right) could buy dead saints' bones at many of the places they visited. They thought these bones had holy powers to help them. Some people tricked pilgrims by selling animal bones instead.

Many saints' bones were kept in boxes shaped like statues.

Peddlers, pilgrims, knights and other travellers

Even in European countries, travel was slow and difficult. But many people still made journeys for all sorts of reasons.

Roads and paths were full of holes and bumps.

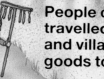

Peddlers

People called peddlers travelled around towns and villages carrying goods to sell.

Pilgrims

People called pilgrims went to pray in places where saints had lived.

Rich people's coach

Knights

Knights and soldiers travelled to fight wars in different countries. There were many wars in the lands near Jerusalem.

Sailing ships took travellers across the sea.

Horses used for carrying things were called pack horses.

Some rich people were carried in a huge travelling box called a litter.

Ladies rode sideways as they wore long skirts.

Rich people

Rich families often had two or more homes. They travelled between them with their servants and friends.

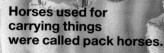

Exploring by sea

Arabs and Turks brought jewels, silks and spices by camel from Eastern countries such as India. They sold them for lots of money to people in Europe. Europeans began to find ways to the East by sea, so they could get these valuable things for themselves.

The first explorers were often frightened. They had to cross unknown seas in small ships. Nobody knew how far they had to go or if they would return.

Sailors stood here to keep watch for land.

Ships were only about 100 feet long. That's about the length of three buses.

An explorer's ship being loaded for a journey.

There was only room for a few animals. They were soon killed and eaten.

Proving the world was round

Many people still thought the world was flat (see page 84). Long sea journeys began to show that the world was round like an orange. This was finally proved when Magellan's ship sailed all the way around the world in 1519-1522.

Some explorers' voyages are marked on this globe. ▶

Magellan died on the way but his ship carried on.

Columbus meant to sail around the world to India in 1492. He landed in the West Indies by mistake.

Vasco da Gama sailed around Africa in 1497.

They took lots of salted pork, biscuits and water to eat and drink. Some took animals so they could have fresh meat at first.

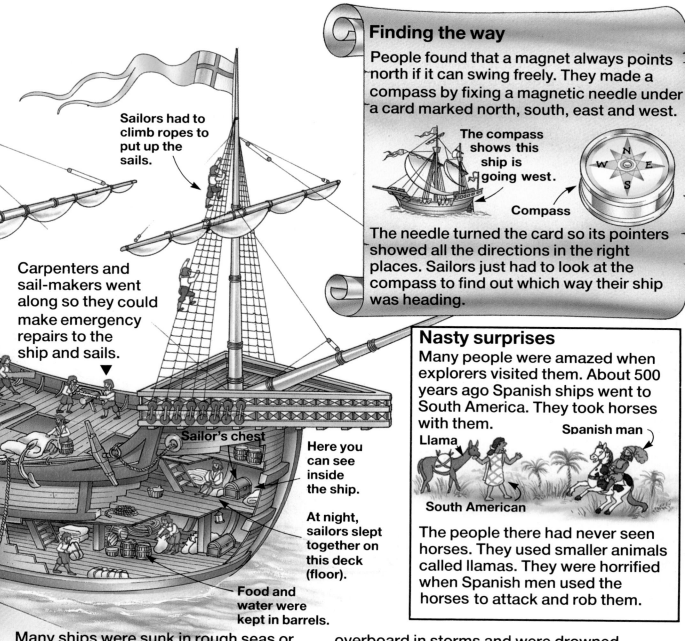

Sailors had to climb ropes to put up the sails.

Carpenters and sail-makers went along so they could make emergency repairs to the ship and sails. ▼

Sailor's chest

Here you can see inside the ship.

At night, sailors slept together on this deck (floor).

Food and water were kept in barrels.

Finding the way

People found that a magnet always points north if it can swing freely. They made a compass by fixing a magnetic needle under a card marked north, south, east and west.

The compass shows this ship is going west.

Compass

The needle turned the card so its pointers showed all the directions in the right places. Sailors just had to look at the compass to find out which way their ship was heading.

Nasty surprises

Many people were amazed when explorers visited them. About 500 years ago Spanish ships went to South America. They took horses with them.

Llama

Spanish man

South American

The people there had never seen horses. They used smaller animals called llamas. They were horrified when Spanish men used the horses to attack and rob them.

Many ships were sunk in rough seas or wrecked on rocks. Even if a ship got back safely lots of the sailors did not. Some fell overboard in storms and were drowned. Many died of scurvy, an illness caused by not eating fresh food for a long time.

Horse-drawn coaches

Early coaches were heavy and awkward (see page 85). About 300 years ago, coach builders began to make coaches lighter and easier for horses to pull. People made long journeys in them. These often took several days or weeks.

Luggage was strapped on the top.

Here you can see inside the stage-coach.

A guard rode with the driver to help fight off highwaymen (see opposite).

A horn warned that the coach was on the way.

It was cheaper to sit in a basket on the back.

Driver

Only very rich people could afford their own coach. They paid lots of money for elegant coaches. They had servants to drive them.

Passengers climbed these steps to get into the coach.

Stage-coach

Crowded beds

At night, stage-coaches stopped at an inn where passengers could sleep. In some inns, people had to share a bed with one or even two strangers. They had to share with bedbugs and fleas as well.

More people could afford to buy tickets for seats in stage-coaches like the one above. These made regular long journeys.

Stage-coaches got their name because they always made a journey in stages. They stopped every few hours, at inns, to change tired horses for fresh ones.

Horse-drawn boats

Heavy loads such as coal were put on flat boats called barges. These were pulled along rivers by horses on the banks.

Horses could pull heavier loads in barges than they could in carts. People built canals (man-made rivers) so barges could carry goods to places not on rivers.

Difficult and dangerous roads

In many countries, roads were rough and difficult to travel on. Few coaches could go faster then 7½ miles per hour.

Some roads had huge stones, and puddles deep enough to drown in. Many coaches fell over on the rough ground, injuring and sometimes killing the passengers.

The driver flicked the horses with a whip to make them go faster.

The driver steered and stopped the horses by pulling on their reins.

Passengers were often uncomfortable. They sat squashed together. The coach swayed a lot so they bumped against each other.

The horses' tails were cut short to stop them getting tangled in the harness.

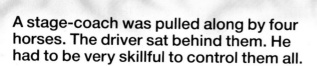

← Harness

A stage-coach was pulled along by four horses. The driver sat behind them. He had to be very skillful to control them all.

Highwaymen

Highwaymen were robbers on horseback. They attacked coaches. They threatened to kill passengers unless they gave up their money and jewels.

Travelling across North America

Before this time, many Europeans had come to live in North America. Most stayed near the East coast where their ships had landed. Then explorers found ways to the West. Families now began to cross America in search of land to farm and live on.

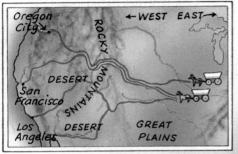

Travellers had to go over mountains, wild plains and deserts. This map shows some of the ways they went.

People travelled in covered wagons pulled by oxen. They took tools and furniture to help them set up their farm homes.

They had to take lots of food and water for the long journey.

A plow for the family's new farm.

Water barrel

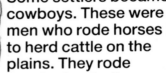

Farm animals followed behind the wagons.

Wheels often broke on the rough ground. Travellers had to know how to mend them.

Cowboys

Some settlers became cowboys. These were men who rode horses to herd cattle on the plains. They rode hundreds of miles each year.

Dangers and difficulties

Sometimes Indians attacked wagons. People travelled in groups so it was easier to fight them off.

Fierce dust storms blew up on the plains. The winds were so strong they overturned some wagons.

Travellers got wagons across rivers by taking their wheels off and letting them float over.

The Pony Express

In 1860, a quick mail service started between the West and the East. This was called the Pony Express. Riders carried the mail on fast ponies. Fresh ponies were kept at stages so riders could change on to them and keep going at full gallop.

Travelling Indians

Indians had lived in teepees on the plains for many years. They moved around to find buffalo to kill for food.

They took their teepees with them when they moved. They folded them and put them on frames. Ponies dragged the frames along.

The cover was made of strong cloth stretched over wooden hoops.

People often had to get out and walk. This made it easier for the wagon to go over rocky ground.

Oxen were strong but slow.

The journey took several months. During that time the wagon was a family's only home. They ate and slept inside it.

Taking the train

In 1869, a railroad was built across America. It was 3,191 miles long. Then people could travel West in comfortable trains.

91

Using steam power

During this time, inventors began to make new machines for people to travel in.

They used steam to power many of these machines.

Early steam trains

Early steam trains seemed very fast to people used to horse-drawn vehicles. Many people were frightened that the speed would kill their passengers. ▼

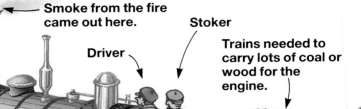

Smoke from the fire came out here.

Driver

Stoker

Trains needed to carry lots of coal or wood for the engine.

Stephenson's 'Rocket'

The wheels ran along iron rails so the train travelled smoothly.

George Stephenson's 'Rocket' was a famous early train. People were amazed at its speed of 30 miles per hour.

Travelling by steam train

A train's carriages were pulled by a steam engine. A man called a stoker shovelled coal or wood to keep a fire going inside it.

This first class carriage has glass windows.

How a steam engine works

A fire heats water in a tank. When the water ▶ boils it turns to steam. The steam rushes along a pipe and pushes a rod called a piston. This is joined to the wheels. The piston turns the wheels as it moves.

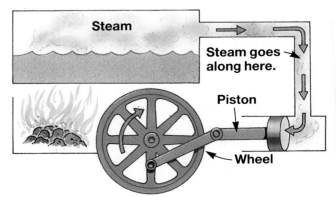

Steam

Steam goes along here.

Piston

Wheel

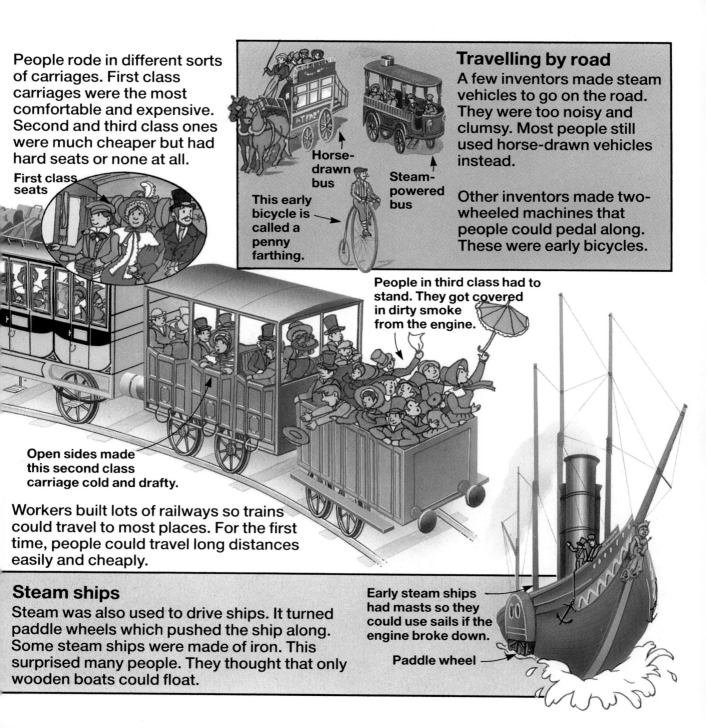

People rode in different sorts of carriages. First class carriages were the most comfortable and expensive. Second and third class ones were much cheaper but had hard seats or none at all.

First class seats

Travelling by road

A few inventors made steam vehicles to go on the road. They were too noisy and clumsy. Most people still used horse-drawn vehicles instead.

Other inventors made two-wheeled machines that people could pedal along. These were early bicycles.

Horse-drawn bus

Steam-powered bus

This early bicycle is called a penny farthing.

People in third class had to stand. They got covered in dirty smoke from the engine.

Open sides made this second class carriage cold and drafty.

Workers built lots of railways so trains could travel to most places. For the first time, people could travel long distances easily and cheaply.

Steam ships

Steam was also used to drive ships. It turned paddle wheels which pushed the ship along. Some steam ships were made of iron. This surprised many people. They thought that only wooden boats could float.

Early steam ships had masts so they could use sails if the engine broke down.

Paddle wheel

Going further and faster

New inventions quickly replaced old ways of travel. Cars were used instead of horses to go over land. Faster ships were used on the sea. Planes and airships flew through the air. People could travel more easily than ever before.

Travelling by car

The very first cars were expensive. Then, in 1909 Henry Ford began to make cheaper cars in efficient factories.

Many people could now afford to buy their own car. Travel became so easy that people often made journeys just for fun.

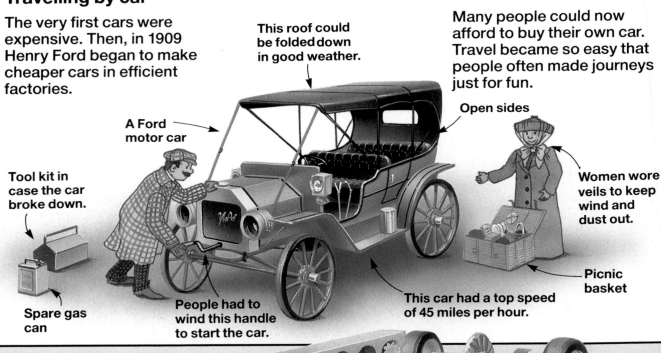

This roof could be folded down in good weather.

A Ford motor car

Open sides

Tool kit in case the car broke down.

Women wore veils to keep wind and dust out.

Spare gas can

People had to wind this handle to start the car.

This car had a top speed of 45 miles per hour.

Picnic basket

Making a car go

Cars were powered with gas engines, a new invention. These are still used in cars today. This is how one works.

Most cars have four cylinders.

Cylinder

Here you can see an explosion inside a cylinder.

Piston

Turning machinery

Gas and air are let into tubes called cylinders. Sparks ignite the gas causing small explosions. The explosions push rods called pistons up and down so they turn machinery in the engine. When the machinery turns the wheels go round.

Flying through the air

Some people had invented flying machines before this time. Most could only hop off the ground. Others like balloons could not be steered very well. ▶

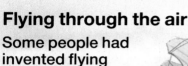
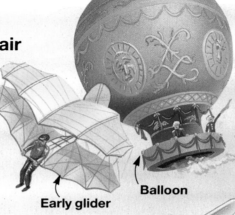

Early glider

Balloon

Airships were the first machines to fly travellers wherever they wanted to go. People sat in cabins below a long gas bag. Propellors pushed the airship along. ▶

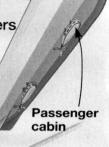

Airship

Passenger cabin

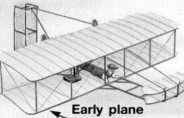

Early plane

Plane in 1936

Helicopter in 1938

The first real airplane was called 'The Flyer'. It was made and flown by Wilbur and Orville Wright in 1903. Later inventors improved on their work.

By 1936, planes could carry passengers at about 180 miles per hour. Today, jet planes carry people at 625 miles per hour to places all over the world.

Another invention, the helicopter, could land in less space than a plane. It is still used to fly people to places in mountains or jungles where planes cannot land.

Moon buggy

Landing craft

Flying to the moon

About 30 years ago, inventors made rockets to take people into space. In 1969, Buzz Aldrin and Neil Armstrong were the first to reach the moon. Since then ten more people have made this 230,000 mile journey.

Sea travel

People began to use submarines like this to explore under the sea. The deepest anyone has been so far is about 6 miles down. ▼

Huge passenger ▲ ships called liners were built. These are still used today. They can carry several hundred people at a time.

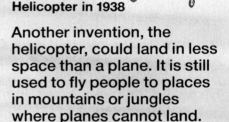

95

Travel facts

Earliest sea journey

★The Aborigine people probably made the first sea journey about 40,000 years ago. They used canoes to cross the sea between New Guinea and Australia.

Sailing submarine

★An early submarine called the Nautilus used a sail when it was on the surface of the sea. When it dived beneath the surface, its crew turned a propeller by hand to move it along.

Devilish bicycles

★ Some people thought early bicycles were a wicked invention. In 1896, an American preacher warned Christians against them. He called them machines 'to trap the feet of the unwary and skin the nose of the innocent'.

Being prepared

★Travellers on early trains were advised to take a first-aid kit with them in case there was an accident.

Early warning

★About 100 years ago in Britain, people thought cars were very dangerous. There was a law that a man had to walk with a red flag in front of each car. This was to warn people that a car was coming.

Rocket car

★In 1979, a car with rocket engines went at a speed of 750 miles per hour. It was called the Budweiser Rocket.

Longest walk

★David Kunst took four and a half years to walk all the way around the world. He finished this 15,000 mile walk in 1974. He wore out 21 pairs of shoes.

First man in a balloon

★Pilâtre de Rozier of France was the first man to fly in a balloon in 1783. The balloon was made by two brothers, Étienne and Joseph Montgolfier.

Flying around the world

★In 1949, Captain James Gallagher flew a plane non-stop around the world. His journey took 94 hours and one minute.

Space dog

★A dog called Laika was the first living creature to go into space. She travelled in a Soviet spacecraft, Sputnik II, in 1957.

Dangerous journeys

★Many stage-coach travellers were so frightened of being killed on their journey that they made out a will before they left.

Index

airplanes, 95
airships, 95
Ancient Egyptians, 4-5,
    28-29, 52-53, 76-77
animal skins, 2, 3, 14, 15, 74,
    75
armor, 7, 10, 24
Aztecs, 63

baking, 53, 58, 63, 71
balloons, 95, 96
barges, 89
baths, 16, 30, 37
beach clothes, 21
bedrooms, 30, 31, 33, 41, 45
beds, 48, 88
beer, 52, 56, 57, 59, 63, 69, 72
bicycles, 18, 45, 93
Bloomer, Amelia, 18
boar, 50, 55, 56, 57, 60
boots, 7, 9, 14, 20, 23
bread, 51, 52, 53, 54, 55, 56,
    58, 59, 63, 69, 71, 72

camels, 79, 81, 86
cans, 68, 70
car clothes, 20, 94
cars, 20, 94, 96
castle, 34-35, 48
caves, 26-27, 74
chain mail, 9, 10, 24
chariots, 77, 78
cheese, 52, 54, 57, 59, 63, 70
chicken, 55, 56, 58, 60, 65
children's clothes, 4, 6, 12,
    15, 19
China, 58, 80-81
chocolate, 63, 65, 72
coaches, 85, 88, 89
coffee, 65, 69, 70
Columbus, 86

compass, 87
cookbooks, 54, 67
coracles, 75
corn, 59, 62, 63, 72
corsets, 12, 16, 18, 19, 20
covered wagons, 90, 91
cowboys, 23, 90
crinolines, 18, 19

da Gama, Vasco, 86
dinner parties, 54, 55, 69
dirtiness, 16, 24
drains, 30, 31, 36
drying food, 53, 56, 58, 70

early travellers, 74-75
earth houses, 43
eggs, 50, 55, 56, 57, 58, 60, 70
electric things, 48, 70, 71
European town house, 36-37
explorers' ships, 86-87

factories, 44, 45, 68, 69, 71
farmers, 50, 56, 58, 67, 72
fire, 18, 24, 26, 30, 31, 33, 44,
    50, 51, 54, 57, 63, 68
fish, 50, 53, 54, 55, 58, 59, 65,
    70, 72
fishing, 50, 53, 56, 58,
Ford, Henry, 94
forks, 55, 66, 69
French cooks, 67
French fashions, 16-17
French nobleman's home,
    40-41
French Revolution, 17, 40
fur, 8, 11, 12, 14, 24
furniture, 29, 39, 42, 45, 48

galleys, 79
gardens, 4, 10, 28, 30, 35, 39,

40, 46, 47, 54, 56, 58, 66
gas cookers, 68, 70
gas engines, 94
glass windows, 34, 36, 38, 46
gods, 31, 77, 79
Great Wall of China, 81

hair, 4, 5, 9, 14, 15, 16, 17, 24
hats, 11, 12, 13, 15, 17, 19, 20,
    21, 23
head-dresses, 10, 11, 12
helicopters, 95
helmets, 7, 9
herbs, 54, 58, 60
highwaymen, 89
horses, 77, 78, 79, 80, 83, 85,
    89, 90, 93
housework, 44, 46
hovercrafts, 95
hunting, 50, 51, 53, 56, 60, 70,
    74
hunting boats, 53, 76
hypocaust, 30

iceboxes, 46, 68, 70
Indians, 14-15, 42, 43, 64, 91
Indian tepees, 42, 43, 91
inns, 79, 88

jeans, 21, 23
jewelry, 2, 3, 5, 8, 9, 14
junks, 81

kayaks, 75
kitchens, 31, 35, 36, 45, 54,
    55, 63, 68, 70
knights, 10
knives, 57, 60, 69

Lent, 59
liners, 95

litters, 79, 85
looms 3, 4, 8, 9
Louis XIV, 16

Magellan, 86
make-up, 4, 5, 7, 16,
mammoth huts, 26
manners, 55, 66
maps, 80, 84
mead, 57, 60
meat, 50, 54, 56, 58, 62, 63,
  65, 69
medieval banquets, 60
medieval clothes, 10, 11
merchants' houses, 38-39
moccasins, 14, 15
mud houses, 28

napkins, 55, 60, 69
necklaces, 3, 14, 15
Nile, 28, 52, 76
North America, 14, 15, 42, 43,
  64, 69, 92-93

oars, 77, 79, 83
oxen, 79, 92, 93

paintings, 27, 29, 31
pease puddings, 59
peddlers, 85
Pepys, Samuel, 65
perfume, 4, 7, 16
petticoats, 14, 15, 18, 21
pigs, 50, 54, 56, 58, 60, 86
pilgrims, 85
Polo, Marco, 84
Pony Express, 91
potatoes, 59, 62, 67, 69
pyramids, 28, 29

rafts, 75
rationing, 71
recipes, 55, 61, 64, 67
roads, 78, 79, 80, 89
Romans, 6-7, 30-31, 54-55,
  78-79
roofs, 28, 30, 32, 33, 37
ruffs, 12, 13

sailors, 62, 68, 76, 82, 83, 86,
  87
sailors' food, 63, 86, 87
sails, 76, 79, 81, 83, 87, 93, 96
salt, 53, 56, 58, 59, 60, 63
Sandwich, Earl of, 67
scurvy, 63, 87
shelters, 26, 48
shoe rules, 11, 24
shoes, 7, 8, 12, 13, 15, 17, 21
shopping, 53, 70
shutters, 31, 36
silk, 6, 13, 14, 15, 16, 17, 22
sleds, 74, 77, 83
soldiers, 7, 20, 21, 78, 80
soup, 59, 63, 69
South America, 23, 62, 63, 75,
  87
spices, 38, 60, 62, 86
stage-coaches, 88-89, 96
steam transport, 91, 92, 93,
  96
Stephenson's Rocket, 92
submarines, 95, 96
sugar, 63, 66, 70
suspension bridge, 80
swaddling, 11

tea, 65, 69
teeth, 3, 17
terraced houses, 44-45
Thanksgiving, 64
things to do, 3, 5, 11, 13, 15,
  27, 41, 43, 47, 57, 69
togas, 6, 7
toilets, 29, 30, 33, 35, 45
trading boats, 76, 77
travelling chairs, 77
trousers, 2, 9, 17, 18, 19
tunics, 6, 7, 8, 9, 10, 11
turbans, 16, 23
turkey, 59, 62, 64

underwear, 6, 9
uniforms, 20, 21

Vikings, 8-9, 32-33, 56-57,
  82-83

waistcoats, 17, 18, 23
water, 28, 31, 32, 34, 37, 44,
  46, 50
weapons, 8, 9
wheels, 74, 90
wigs, 4, 5, 16, 17, 24
Wild West, 42-43
wine, 53, 54. 55, 60, 65
Wright, Wilbur and Orville, 95

Answer

Page 45 – The word is teapot

Printed in Belgium